With his free hand, he stroke

of her hair,

then his kisses ended as gradually as they had begun, in a trail of tiny nibbles along her cheekbone.

When he pulled away, he left her warm and flushed, her pulse rushing. Her cheek nestled against his as he continued to fondle her long hair, the sensation relaxing her.

"Tory," he breathed her name, "I don't ever want you to leave."

"I don't ever want to leave," she admitted without thinking. But almost as soon as the words were out, she recognized their absurdity.

As in the past, the chilly winds of reality came creeping into her fantasy, clearing away the soft, warm clouds of her dream world. She raised her head from his shoulder to look directly into his face.

Brushing a wave of hair from his forehead, she kissed him there, then stepped out of his embrace ...

"Regardless of what I've said, the facts remain unchanged. Come Monday I'll be heading home."

Rand took her gently but firmly by the elbows. "You don't *have* to go on Monday if you don't want to, Tory," he said earnestly ... "I want you near me, Tory. Not a couple of hundred miles away where I can't see you, can't touch you, can't show you how much I care."

Dear Reader,

Welcome to the world of *Great Lakes Romances*TM, a new historical fiction series full of love and adventure, set in bygone days on North America's vast inland waters.

Each book will relay the excitement and thrills of a tale skillfully told, but will not contain explicit sex, swearing, or gratuitous violence.

We invite you to tell us what you would like most to read about in *Great Lakes Romances*TM. For your convenience, we have included a survey form at the back of the book. Please fill it out and send it to us, and be sure to watch for the next book in the series, coming in Spring 1990.

Thank you for being a part of *Great Lakes Romances*TM!

Sincerely,
The Publishers

P.S. Author Donna Winters loves to hear from her readers. You can write her at P.O. Box 177, Caledonia, MI 49316.

MACKINAC

by
DONNA WINTERS

Great Lakes Romances™

Bigwater Publishing
Caledonia, Michigan

To Fred,
the one who makes my dreams come true

Notes and Acknowledgments

Mackinac is pronounced **Mack**inaw.

I would like to thank the following people for their assistance and advice in preparation of this work:

Howard Creswick for the map of Michigan and BP logo
Art Jacobs for artistic insights
Hank Sefcovic for legal advice
Chuck Ward for computer system consultations

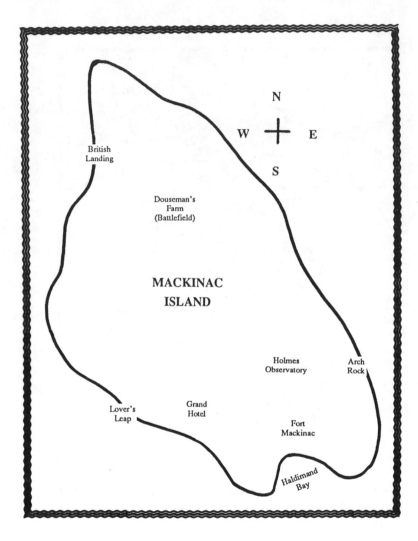

Chapter 1

Mackinac Island - August 1895

Pressing against the bow rail of the *Algomah*, twenty-year-old Victoria Whitmore held her straw hat in place over her neatly coiled dark hair. The ferry's engine vibrated gently beneath her feet, pulsing through her as though she were a part of the vessel. Amidships, black clouds of coal smoke from the tall stack spiced the air.

Victoria stood in a throng of passengers on the bow, among them, a retired old sea dog with a slightly shaggy salt and pepper beard. Not given to pretense, he had introduced himself to her only moments before as Scotty, and wasted no time informing her that he had spent nearly his entire life on the Great Lakes.

"I suppose you've been to Mackinac Island dozens of times," Victoria commented, hoping some conversation would help ease her taut nerves. The overnight train ride from Grand Rapids, the too-rich cream served with the oatmeal on which she had breakfasted in the elegant dining car, and her dread of facing a creditor to demand payment had already wreaked havoc with her stomach.

"Yes, ma'am, Miss ... ?"

"Whitmore. Victoria Whitmore."

"Like I was sayin', Miss Whitmore, I've crossed the straits many a time since I was a boy o' six. This your first trip to the island?" he asked, his bushy brow rising to deepen the grooves in his weathered forehead.

Victoria nodded.

"Thought so. Don't like ferries much, do you, Miss Whitmore?"

"I'm afraid not, Scotty." It wasn't exactly the truth, but she was unwilling to explain the real cause of her worry.

"Fair sailin' today. This is 'bout the calmest these waters get. Pretty soon, the cap'n 'll ease this old gal in at the dock so gentle you'll hardly know we're there."

She gazed off in the direction of Mackinac Island and tried to exercise patience as she watched the emerald blur grow distinct with recognizable features. On its southern shore, Haldimand Bay opened along graceful curves, taking in its embrace a canoe gliding across shimmering waters, guided by the deft strokes of its steersman. A tiny dinghy skimmed along behind a luxurious private yacht, and a double-masted Mackinac boat flew its gaff-rigged mainsails and triangular jib in the steady north-easterly breeze.

"Look there, Miss Whitmore. Old Fort Mackinac." Scotty pointed to a long, white wall. Just as the brilliant sun cut multi-faceted diamonds into the harbor's quiet surface, it caused the limestone fortress high atop the imposing East Bluff to glow softly.

"Over to the right, at the top o' the ramp, is the South Sally Port, and to the left o' that, the officers' wood quarters, and the officers' stone quarters," he explained.

The pristine white structures peered down on a shoreline jammed with hotels and storehouses, shanties and fishnet dryers, and a series of docks jutting out like the stiff wooden fingers of a cigar-store Indian.

"I used to like watchin' the soldiers drill on the parade field at Fort Mackinac, but they're mostly gone now. All but eleven of 'em. Won't be the same on the island without 'em," he lamented. "You be sure an take a look at the fort while you're on the island, though, Miss Whitmore. And don't neglect Arch Rock, 'n Sugarloaf, 'n Holmes Observatory."

"They all sound interesting," Victoria admitted, "but I'm not sure I'll have time." She pointed to a long, white edifice coming clearer into view west of the fort. "That must be Grand Hotel."

"Aye. Sure 'nough 'tis. Grand Lady o' the island, I like to call her."

Above the shoreline's collection of mismatched structures, the hotel was surely the most fascinating of all. Like a proud monarch, she sat ensconced on the throne of a grassy hill, her long rows of windows looking out over the comings and goings of the harbor below. Victoria trembled with anticipation at the thought of claiming her room and demanding of its manager payment of his overdue account with her father's furniture factory.

The ferry was coming into dock now, nudging it gently as Scotty had predicted. "Well, Miss Whitmore, I'll be on my way now. You have a nice vacation."

Victoria's attention shifted to the commotion dockside. Amidst the shouts of dockworkers, and securing of the *Algomah's* heavy lines, the ferry claimed her berth. Victoria descended the crowded gangway in close company of an obviously lovestruck young couple. Honeymooners, she concluded. Thoughts of marriage, romance, or even gentlemen callers, she suddenly realized, had been far from her mind in the four years she had been working for her father, ever since her mother's death.

She pulled her skirt in close, making her way past casks and crates, barrels and hogsheads, kegs and chests that lined the bustling pier. The stench of fish competed with the odor of manure to taint the balmy air, while a steam engine hissed away on a neighboring dock, working a derrick to load coal onto a waiting steamer. Wagons and drays jockeyed for positions along the waterfront.

She stepped deftly around mounds of hay-flecked excrement and made her way to a line of waiting hacks.

"Hudson's Tours, finest coaches on the island!" one of the drivers called to her.

"Ride with Dependable Dan, and see Mackinac in safety and comfort!" hawked another. "How 'bout it, miss? Take you past Robinson's Folly, Arch Rock and Sugarloaf, 'round to Holmes Observatory, then on over to the fort, where you can feast your eyes on the most bee-you-tee-ful scenery of the Midwest." He whipped off his hat, and with a sweeping motion, bade her step aboard his rig.

"No, thank you, sir," Victoria responded, hurrying toward a two-horse rig with the words *Grand Hotel* emblazoned on the side.

Its driver was tall and brawny with rosy splotches on fair cheeks that gave him a gentle look in spite of his size. He patted his mare's nose and slipped her a lump of sugar, chuckling at her eagerness for the treat, then offered the gelding of the pair the same. Facing Victoria, he hooked a thumb beneath the suspenders that followed the curve of his large belly. "Bound for Grand Hotel?" he asked cheerfully.

"Yes, sir."

He gave her a hand up to the empty second seat. "There are a few more coming, then we'll be off. M' name's Big John," he explained.

Victoria settled onto the polished leather upholstery. "I'm Victoria Whitmore."

"Pleased to make y'r acquaintance." He touched the brim of his straw hat. "I trust you'll enjoy y'r stay."

Victoria smiled pleasantly. No point explaining she had not come seeking enjoyment.

Within minutes the surrey had filled with passengers. Big John's spirited team progressed deftly through the congested Main Street traffic, and up the long incline of busy Cadotte Avenue, reluctant to pull over and let a trap pass. Sitting pretty beneath her parasol was an elegantly ruched, flounced, and bonneted society matron, accompanied by several similarly outfitted friends.

Victoria noted that Big John touched the brim of his hat in deference to the passing entourage. "That's Mrs. Palmer, queen bee o' Chicago society, 'n some o' her friends, likely on their way to a luncheon somewheres," he explained over his shoulder. "She's just about the most charming lady ever to visit Mackinac Island. Why, I heard tell she even charmed Congress out of thirty-six thousand dollars for the Women's Building at the Columbian Exposition in Chicago two years back!"

Even Victoria, as far removed from high society as one could be, knew that Bertha Honorè Palmer had ensured the success of the Chicago World Exposition of 1893 by traveling to Europe beforehand to solicit participation in the event.

Victoria's attempt to view the famous personage from behind was rewarded with a glimpse of her pale pink parasol.

Moments later, Big John turned left at the Grand Hotel, passed in front of its portico, which ran the entire length of the establishment, and stopped beneath the porte cochère.

"Here y' be, folks." He jumped down and held Victoria's elbow as she alighted from the carriage.

"Thank you kindly, John." She handed him a tip.

"And thank *you*, Miss Whitmore." He assisted the others, then climbed aboard again, clucked to his team and drove off.

Victoria was almost sorry to see him leave, for now she must face the task she had been dreading for days. She smoothed the wrinkles from the skirt of her navy blue serge suit and briskly mounted the front steps. Facing the imposing double door, she paused a moment to admire the decorative window above, its delicate framework spreading like the ribs of a fan. Catching her breath, she stepped inside, entering the office and rotunda.

Here, rows of fluted columns stretched upward to a high, vaulted ceiling. In the midst of their grand parade hung a magnificent chandelier, each of its brass arms curving gracefully outward to support a lighted globe. A wide staircase rose gently to the floor above, and to the east was a broad hallway covered with an intricately patterned Turkey carpet.

She moved through the rotunda. The muffled conversation of two businessmen, and soft rustling of a society matron's skirts came to her as guests of Grand Hotel passed by, bringing in their wake the heavy fragrance of expensive French perfume.

Further along, in the lobby, was a scattering of straight-backed chairs, the very same for which her father had not been paid, and Victoria determined then and there she would not leave the island until compensation had been made.

With renewed purpose, she strode toward the reception desk. On the floor before it lay a Turkey carpet rich in reds and blues, and across the surface of the counter, a thick slab of genuine marble. Displayed prominently on a stand was the guest register, and filling the wall behind the desk were row upon row of mail slots, each with its own key hook.

A hotel clerk, a young man of about twenty, approached Victoria before she could ring the bell. His smile, in pleasant contrast to the formality of the establishment, was unpretentious. "Can I help you?"

"I have a reservation in the name of Miss Victoria Whitmore."

"One moment, please." He shuffled through the "w's" in a file box, removing a neatly typed card. "Miss Victoria Whitmore," he read. "I have a sleeping apartment for you for tonight only."

"That's correct."

"Sign here, please." He rotated the guest register on its stand until it faced her, and pointed to the next empty line on the half-filled page. She penned her name with slightly shaky strokes, adding the date, August 12. As he retrieved a key from one of the hooks behind him, Victoria estimated there must be at least four hundred rooms to the establishment.

"I'll have Robert show you to your room. It's on the second floor to the right of the stairs. Your luggage will be delivered the moment it arrives." In response to his subtle gesture, a uniformed bellboy of about eighteen stepped up. His sandy hair looked as though it had been streaked by the sun, and a touch of amber lent warmth to his brown eyes.

His efficiency had almost made her forget her reason for coming. "Excuse me, Robert. Before I take my room, may I ask where I might find Mr. Bartlett? I'm to meet with him today."

"Certainly. I'll take you to his office." The young man led her to a room behind the reception desk.

Viewed through the open door, a gentleman occupied an oak desk, his head bent in concentration over a typewriter keyboard where he tapped on the keys with a steady, moderate rhythm.

Robert cleared his throat. "Excuse me. Mr. Donovan, Miss Whitmore." The gentleman, who appeared to be in his mid-thirties, rose from his desk, pushing back a wave of hair the shade of fall pumpkins. To Victoria, Robert explained, "Mr. Donovan is Mr. Bartlett's assistant."

Victoria offered a coin to the bellboy. "Thank you, Robert."

He dipped his head, and hurried away.

Victoria strode up to the desk with a confidence she didn't feel. "I'm here representing Whitmore Furniture Manufactory. I'm to see Mr. Bartlett today."

"Miss Whitmore?" Hurriedly, the assistant opened the appointment book on his desk. As he searched the pages, Victoria noted a closed door behind him labeled "Rand Bartlett-Hotel Manager."

"I'll just announce myself, Mr. Donovan," Victoria said, stepping past him.

"Mr. Bartlett isn't in his office at the moment," the assistant stated firmly. The pale hollows of his cheeks became suffused with ruddy patches.

Victoria tried the door and found it locked. "Where is he? I sent word several days ago that I'd be arriving this afternoon to meet with him.

Didn't you make a note of it when you received my letter?"

"Your letter was very vague. It made no mention of a specific time, only that you'd be here this afternoon." He picked up her missive that lay on the open page. "Mr. Bartlett is a very busy man. The earliest he could see you would be half past four this afternoon."

"Half past four? Not sooner?" she asked accusingly.

"I'm afraid not. At the moment, Mr. Bartlett is not even on the island. He's due to return late this afternoon. I'll tell him to expect you." He ushered her from the room.

"Until later, Mr. Donovan."

Disappointed, Victoria crossed the lobby to the grand staircase. No need to hurry, she thought, now that she had two hours to wait--two long hours that would most certainly be filled with worry and dread. She doubted that even *The Adventures of Huckleberry Finn,* her favorite novel which she had been rereading on the train, could take her mind off the impending meeting.

Mounting the first three steps, she turned to take in the beauty and magnificence of the rotunda. She might as well enjoy these elegant surroundings while she could. Soon enough, she would be back on the ferry, homeward bound.

Yes. Soon enough she would have payment in hand and hurry home to keep the creditors from foreclosing on her father's business one more time.

Other guests moved at a leisurely pace past white columns toward parlors and shops off the wide hallway. How different from theirs Victoria knew her stay at Grant Hotel would be! She had come, not out of a desire for relaxation, but out of the necessity to obtain the payment that would once again put her father's business in the black.

In the lobby, men sat conversing in the very walnut chairs her father had shipped three months ago. Functional they were, yet each chair was graced with a hand-carved hotel insignia in an oval medallion on the center of its back. Just such painstaking detail had earned Jacob Whitmore a reputation high enough to merit an order from this, Michigan's most famous and elegant resort.

Unfortunately, fame and elegance had not made the establishment the state's most lucrative hostelry. Their unpaid bill, one of many, Victoria suspected, had made necessary her unusual excursion to obtain the payment that would provide the lifeblood for her father's furniture manufactory.

She continued up the stairs, turning right until she reached her room. The key worked easily in the polished brass lock, and the door opened to reveal that her luggage had arrived.

Down the hall, Victoria heard another door open.

"Well, hello!" a cheery voice greeted.

Victoria turned to take in the sight of a pretty, petite, fair-haired young lady whose frilly yellow dress gave her the appearance of a pixie-angel.

"I'm Lily Atwood. So you're my new next-door neighbor, Miss ... ?"

"Victoria Whitmore. Pleased to meet you, Miss Atwood." She offered her hand.

Lily placed her small hand in Victoria's, exhibiting an unexpectedly firm grip. "Please, call me Lily. 'Miss Atwood' makes me feel so old. I'm only eighteen, for heaven's sake."

"All of that?" Victoria smiled. "I'd have put you at sixteen, you're so tiny."

"I know. My pudgy cheeks don't help any. I still look like a child, but I'm a mature woman, really. A debutante, formally and properly launched into society, as it were." She sucked in her cheeks and threw back her head and shoulders, taking a few steps down the hall.

Turning arrogantly, she managed to reach Victoria's door before bursting into giggles. "Hard to believe Mother and Father spent thousands of dollars on governesses to teach me such sophistication. Oh, well. I pretend all those deportment and diction lessons made a difference when I'm in Manhattan. But for now, who cares?" She half-whispered, "This is just about the crudest place I've ever lived."

Victoria suppressed her shock. How could anyone, even the wealthy from the East Coast, consider Grand Hotel crude?

Lily continued. "I'm only here for the month of August, thank goodness, staying with my Aunt Agatha in what she says is one of the best suites in the hotel." She glanced at the trunk in Victoria's room, and as if invited, stepped through the open door. "I'll be glad to help you unpack, Tory."

Victoria followed her into the room. "Pardon? What did you call me?"

"Tory. That's your nickname, isn't it? I could call you Victoria, or

Miss Whitmore, but those hardly seem appropriate between friends. You *will* be my friend, won't you? I mean, for the past week this end of the hall has been utterly spare of young ladies my age." She clasped her hands with glee. "Oh, I can't tell you how pleased I am that you're here." She crossed the room to Victoria's trunk. "I hope you'll be staying awhile. What with the big party coming up on the weekend, and all." She unbuckled the lid, opened the trunk and lifted out the jacket belonging to a gray pinstripe suit.

Victoria reached for the jacket, appalled at Lily's bold intrusion. "I'll hang that up, if you don't mind. By the way, I've never in my life been called Tory, or Vicky, or any other shortened version of my name. And I'm staying only for tonight. I have business to attend to this afternoon."

"Well, you've certainly brought the wardrobe for it, Tory, I mean, Victoria," Lily responded, completely nonplussed. She held up the skirt that went with the pinstriped jacket. "I'm so glad we'll be friends, even if it is just for a little while. Couldn't you get the hotel to give you the room until the weekend? It promises to be great fun. Everyone's talking about it. There's Field Day, with all those races and competitions. Everyone's going to be here, they say. All those important people from Chicago my aunt keeps telling me about. You know, those innkeepers and shopkeepers. I can't quite remember their names."

"You mean Mrs. Palmer?"

"Yes, she's one of them. And that family with the big department store. Marsh and something ... it reminded me of the outdoors."

"Marshall Field?"

"That's it, Marshall Field." She joined Victoria at the closet, hanging the skirt beside its mate. "Then there are those horrid meat people. They're coming, too. I think I shall just keep my distance from them. After all, how can a decent person approve of a man who makes a living--a fortune, really--by slaughtering innocent animals?"

"What business did you say your family was in, Lily?"

"Father's a financier. What about yourself? You *did* say it was business that brought you here." Lily waltzed over to the dresser and primped in front of the large oval mirror, rearranging the fuzzy yellow curls on her forehead.

"Furniture." Victoria reached into her trunk for a shirtwaist, and waited for her one-word response to bring a new flow of conversation from the loquacious Lily.

"Well, you've come to the right place. Grand Hotel must need lots of furniture. I bet you could talk them into giving you a generous order--"

"They've already given me a generous order. It's the payment they're stingy on."

Lily's head snapped around. "You don't say!" Her words were hushed. Too late, Victoria realized she had provided the talkative girl with a choice morsel of gossip. "So you're here, all by yourself, to collect on an overdue account. How absolutely ... *independent* of you. I'm outrageously jealous. My Aunt Agatha will barely let me out of her sight." In a whisper, she added, "Old Eagle-eye, I call her."

She continued, sotto-voce. "Back in Manhattan, my beau and I had planned to elope, but Mother found out." She rolled her eyes. "As my punishment, I've been banished to this faraway island for the summer." A haughty laugh escaped her. "I guess Mother figured a month away from Blake would do me good, but with all her social commitments, she's too busy to keep track of me. She knew Aunt Agatha wouldn't falter in her duties as my warden, though. I'm virtually under house arrest, you know."

Victoria suppressed a smile. "I can think of a lot of young ladies who would be happy to trade places with you."

"Friends of yours, you mean? Where are you from, anyway?"

"Grand Rapids."

"Grand Rapids? Where's that? Somewhere in Michigan, isn't it?"

"It's about 250 miles south of here, and a little to the west."

"Now, with all due respect, Tory ... Victoria ... I ask you, what would your Grand Rapids friends know about being deprived of a summer of regattas and parties and cotillions in Newport to spend lonely days and nights on this remote island?"

Victoria laughed. "You're right. My friends would know nothing at all of your hardship, being deprived of access to Newport society for the summer, but they'd think a month at Grand Hotel on Mackinac was the next best thing to heaven compared to a summer in Grand Rapids."

"Pooh. They're welcome to it."

As Victoria hung the last of her things in the closet, Lily sauntered across the room to inspect, pushing aside one hanger at a time. "Pretty conservative in your choice of styles, aren't you? Don't you ever socialize? There's not a party frock in here. Just a practical suit, and one skirt and shirtwaist that might get you into the dining room."

"I told you, I'm here on business, not to socialize."

"I'll change that. You'll be seated with Auntie and me at dinner tonight. I'll see to the arrangements. And afterward, we'll talk her into a stroll along the veranda. One trip down the porch will tire her out so she'll be contented to sit in a rocker, then we can take the length of it on our own. Maybe you'll even catch the eye of some young entrepreneuer."

Victoria checked the watch pinned to her lapel. Though her appointment was over an hour away, she was eager to have her room to herself. "Goodness, time is slipping by. If you'll excuse me, I have to prepare for my business appointment this afternoon." She ushered Lily toward the door.

"I'm sure you don't need any help. In fact, it looks to me like you're all ready to demand your due, what with that stark blue suit you're wearing." Lily paused inside the door to pluck at the fabric of Victoria's sleeve.

"I need to wash up." She gently nudged the young girl into the hall and began to close the door, but Lily placed her hand on the jamb.

"You'll find your bathroom over there." She nodded to a narrow door directly across from Victoria's room. "Isn't this absolutely outrageous, having to go across the hall to use the necessary? I understand the men who built this place didn't want to take up any of the prime hotel frontage with plumbing. Such cheapskates. They must have been single, because I'm sure their wives would have set them straight and never allowed such an arrangement."

"Thanks for telling me about the washroom. I'll see you later." Victoria closed the door to within an inch of Lily's hand.

"Ta-ta."

The fingers disappeared, and Victoria latched and chained her door.

Lily. What a chatterbox! She's spoiled and curious as a cat and--Victoria chuckled softly--*and more interesting than any of my pastel friends back in Grand Rapids.*

That city seemed a world away. The little shop where her father labored over hand-carved chair backs, their cramped apartment above it, the Union Station where he had seen her off just yesterday--it hardly seemed possible she would be going back there after only a day on Mackinac Island.

Not only was it a possibility, it was a necessity. She could ill afford this excursion, short as it was. On the other hand, she couldn't let Grand Hotel delay payment, either. By week's end, the bank would be clamoring for money. They might force her father out of business if he didn't come through.

She opened the portfolio and withdrew copies of the purchase order, her billing notices, and the statements she had sent over the past three months since he had completed the order for a hundred straight-backed chairs and two hand-carved desks. The most recent statement included her plea for speedy payment, but it, too, had been ignored. She jogged the papers together and slid them back into the leather folio. In an hour she would have her chance, in person, to bring pressure on the hotel manager to pay up his account.

Taking toiletries from her valise, she stepped across the hall. The bathroom did indeed look out on the uninteresting backyard of the grounds.

When she had washed the grit from her face, brushed her hair and rearranged it in a chignon, she returned to her room to take a good look at the view from the front.

There, before her, stretched a panorama of village and waterfront, bay and lake, deep azure blue waters beneath pale baby blue sky, and a few cottony clouds for good measure. She opened the window wide and inhaled the air coming in off the straits, clear air that doctors had been recommending to patients for decades. It really *was* cleaner, fresher, balmier than the hot, sticky, smelly atmosphere of the city in August.

"Might as well enjoy it now," she told herself. "It's your only chance, and you've paid well for the privilege."

Twenty-five minutes past four. Victoria took a clothes brush to the hem of her skirt to rid it of the dust that had accumulated there from traveling. From her small bottle of hyacinth toilet water, she allowed herself one tiny drop behind each ear before tucking her portfolio under her arm.

Mr. Donovan was again tapping away at the keys of his typewriter when she entered his office. She stood before his desk. "Is Mr. Bartlett in, now?"

He glanced at his wall clock. "Half past four already? I spoke with Mr. Bartlett a few minutes ago. He's expecting you and should be here any moment. Please be seated."

She perched on one of the straightbacked chairs from her father's manufactory.

Mr. Donovan resumed his typing, muttering to himself whenever he hit a wrong key.

Victoria mentally reviewed the approach she would use to extract payment. She must succeed, and succeed this very day. She could not afford to remain at Grand Hotel for another night, or anywhere else on the island, for that matter.

The hands of the clock seemed to move at an intolerably slow pace, yet fifteen minutes passed, and still there was no sign of Mr. Rand Bartlett.

Victoria grew restless. Mr. Donovan, buried in his work, paid her no mind. She flicked an invisible piece of lint from the padded shoulder of her suit jacket then stepped up to his desk, clearing her throat.

"It is now 4:45. You promised me Mr. Bartlett would be here at half past. Where is he?"

The man ran his fingers through already-tousled hair and rose from his desk. "I'm sorry, Miss Whitmore. I can't imagine what's keeping him."

At the sound of approaching footsteps, Victoria turned to face a solidly built man in his thirties.

"Victoria Whitmore? Rand Bartlett." He spoke rapidly. "Sorry I'm late." He shook her hand.

His steady grip caused her heartbeat to quicken. The dancing lights in his hazel eyes seemed to take in everything at once. He exuded the vitality and youth of a man ten years his junior.

Standing but a few inches taller than her five-foot-six, the expanse of chest and shoulders beneath the light gray pinstripe suit made up in girth what Rand Bartlett lacked in height. His was a compact form born of exercise and sport rather than fatty pounds gained from the popular pastime of nearly continuous eating and drinking.

She cleared her throat and extracted her hand from his, attempting to regain some distance, and to dispel the tingling sensation that had set her nerves dancing from her toes up to the very roots of her hair. "Mr.

Bartlett--"

"Call me Rand, or Slick, if you like. That's what my friends call me."
A broad smile, at once magnetic and mischievous, played beneath his
neatly trimmed mustache.

Victoria struggled desperately to ignore his charm, and sternly reminded herself that she had come a great distance at considerable expense to meet with this man because he had disregarded her correspondence. "Mr. Bartlett, we're barely acquainted, and such familiarity is
clearly out of place," she insisted, "and, furthermore--"

"But you are my guest, and surely *some* familiarity is called for under
the circumstances. After all, it's my duty as Grand Hotel manager to
ensure you an enjoyable stay."

"My stay would already have been much more enjoyable had you not
kept me waiting for our scheduled appointment."

He seemed not to hear. Turning instead to his assistant, he pulled a
folded paper from his inside jacket pocket and handed it to him. "Please
give this to Mr. Munson and ask him to investigate the situation immediately, Mr. Donovan."

Addressing Victoria again, he said, "Miss Whitmore, come with me.
I'm on my way to check on the orchestra. They're just concluding an
afternoon concert on the veranda, and I want to speak with them about
the entertainment for tomorrow evening."

She found herself heading across the rotunda and toward the grand
portico propelled by his hand at the small of her back. Nevertheless,
Victoria was determined to talk business.

She withdrew a billing notice from her portfolio. "Mr. Bartlett, I've
come to see you about your overdue account with Whitmore Furniture,"
she stated unequivocally, rattling the page in front of him.

He removed his hand from her back and lengthened his stride. "I'm
sure I sent payment months ago," he answered, pulling away from her.

In her narrow skirt, Victoria had to struggle to keep pace with him.
Abruptly, he came to a halt just inside the grand entrance, turning to face
her so quickly she nearly collided with him.

He cupped his hand around hers, lowering it, and the bill, to her side.
She thought to protest, but his warm smile disarmed her.

"Let's discuss this later, shall we? Say, over a picnic lunch tomorrow.
That will give me time to check with my accountant on the matter." His

words flowed as smooth as honey over hot biscuits.

She flicked her hand free of his touch. "Impossible. I won't be here for lunch tomorrow. I can't afford your hotel's rates for another night." Her volume rose. "I need payment, Mr. Bartlett, and I need it today, or the entire Whitmore Furniture operation is in jeopardy. Do you understand?" Her heart was pounding, and she could feel her face coloring with anger and indignation.

The charming smile beneath his carefully trimmed mustache remained firmly in place. "Then tomorrow night is on the house. Meet me at the Holmes Observatory. A carriage will be waiting for you in the porte cochère at noon. I'd offer to drive you there myself, but I have other matters to attend to beforehand and will have to meet you there. Until tomorrow, Miss Whitmore." With a wave and a wink, he stepped through the doorway and vanished in the crowd mingling on the veranda.

Chapter 2

Hot currents of anger surged along Victoria's spine, and she was certain her pale complexion had suffused with enough color to match the red in the staircase runner. She had to restrain herself from racing up the grand staircase to the second floor, then down the hallway to her room. With a turn of the key, she flung open the door, tossing her portfolio onto the dresser top on her way across the room to the bed. She sat down so hard the bed frame creaked, then she let out an exasperated sigh. "A picnic! Of all places to discuss an overdue account!" She pounded the mattress with her fist.

"Were you talking to me?"

Victoria's head popped up at the sound of the familiar voice. "Lily. I didn't know you were there."

"Just thought I'd stop by and see how it went. No luck, huh?" She crossed the room, alighting on the only chair. "What are you going to do now?" she asked, leaning forward conspiratorially. "Sue him?"

Rising, Victoria laughed. "I could hardly afford a lawyer for *that*."

"You could afford one on contingency," she offered eagerly. "He would only get paid if you do."

Victoria strolled to the dresser and opened her portfolio. "Oh, no. I'm going to collect this payment myself. Papa's company can't afford to share part of it with a lawyer."

"You're really dedicated to your papa and his enterprise, aren't you?" Lily asked, as if the idea were unusual.

"He's all I've got, and I'm all he's got, except for his tiny furniture shop. Mother died of pneumonia when I was sixteen. She used to take care of all of Papa's billing, but I had to learn how to do it after she was gone.

"Papa's shop nearly burned down a few weeks after we buried Mother. Papa was so full of grief, he had let the bills go, and one day the gas company turned off the gas.

"He lit kerosene lanterns in his workshop that afternoon. As usual, he was absorbed in his work, and he accidentally knocked one of them over and started a fire. The shop, and our tiny upstairs apartment nearly turned to cinders." She did not add that she had been on her way home from school when the fire broke out, and her help in extinguishing the flames had prevented the building from turning into a pile of ashes.

"I was very upset for a long time after Mother died." Victoria fidgeted with the pages in her portfolio, trying to forget how very depressed she had become at the time of her loss. "I'm certain Mother's death resulted from her inability to fight off respiratory disease. Her lungs had been weakened by the years she had spent early in her marriage working alongside Papa in a cold, drafty workshop. She was ever devoted to Papa, helping to keep his business alive when he was too poor to hire workers or heat the building properly.

"Mother spent twelve hours a day for weeks on end sanding chairs, desks, bed frames Papa had turned on his lathe and hand-carved with the rose patterns he designed. Mother stained them, then rubbed on the varnish and wax by hand." Victoria's mouth curved upward. "Papa used to say she achieved a richer finish because her fingers were smaller than his and she seemed better able to work the finishing coats into the grain."

Victoria herself, once she was old enough to be of help, had spent many an evening staining and finishing alongside her parents in a shop heavy with the odor of varnish. She remembered the feel of the oily substances on her hands and automatically inspected her fingernails for traces of walnut brown. Years had passed since she had hand-rubbed a chair with wood stain but she could recall it as if it were last week when she had struggled to keep Whitmore Furniture from fading into debt-ridden oblivion.

She would not share this part of her past with Lily, who had been born into a life of abundance. Victoria wondered for a fleeting moment what Lily's life must be like. She had never met a debutante before, but she had heard about them once from Abby Thompson, her high school chum. Abby's cousin in Chicago had been presented to society last year, and Abby had told Victoria every detail of her cousin's boastful letters, including descriptions of gowns, a dozen or more new ones made for the "season." Surely one so wealthy had no idea what life would be like for a girl of meager circumstances. Victoria could hardly expect Lily to understand a desperate financial situation.

Neither did Victoria admit she had considered dropping out of school following her mother's death. The grieving girl's grades had slipped, and she had lost sight of her need for attending. Her bookkeeping classes became her only reason for staying in school.

"Sounds to me like you and your Papa have suffered your share of setbacks." Lily's thoughtful observation brought Victoria back to the present.

"When the fire occurred," Victoria continued, "I realized I would have to learn to take care of the accounts. I hadn't known until then how little inclination Papa had to tend to the chore. He just seemed to bury himself in his work for the next two years."

"Your daddy must be very good at what he does, to have an account with Grand Hotel," Lily commented. "This place isn't my cup of tea, but Auntie tells me it's the best in the Midwest."

Victoria sat on her bed again, facing Lily. "Papa's built a reputation for himself as a master carver over the last twenty-four years. He inspects absolutely everything personally before he ships it. Usually he does small orders. A desk and chair, perhaps, or a dining room suite for one of the wealthier families in Grand Rapids. We thought he'd really hit it big when Grand Hotel sent us this order. How ironic that their lack of payment could spell his doom!"

"So what did Mr. Bartlett say? You were gone nearly half an hour. Surely he offered you a dozen excuses in that time."

After Victoria had shared the content of her conversation with the hotel manager, she ended by saying, "I'll tell you, Lily, he's slippery as butter on an ear of hot corn, and I'm so angry I let him put me off, I could just spit."

"But you won't, because you're a perfect lady about everything. You'll go to the picnic, and even get to stay for the dance tomorrow night. Relax, Tory ... Victoria. There's nothing more you can do about it, so you might as well enjoy yourself. And you can have meals with Auntie and me!"

"Thank you, Lily. It does look as if I'll be staying longer than the one night. And I'd like to eat with someone I know."

"What fun!" With a swirl of her flounced skirt, she headed for the door, pausing in the mirror to scowl at her reflection and rearrange the blond tendrils at her plump cheeks. "We'll come by for you at six. Ta-ta."

Dinner in Grand Hotel's two-story dining room proved an experience in itself. White Irish damask linen napkins stood at each place, having been arranged in the shape of a cone with a pointed top. The fabric, when Victoria unfolded it, felt more luxurious to the touch than any she'd ever known. Enough pieces of gleaming sterling silver were laid at Victoria's place for at least three meals. She was quite troubled at first over which pieces to use, then she remembered advice her mother had once given her to work from the outside, and watch how others chose their silver. Hungry though she was, she waited patiently for Lily's aunt to begin before picking up her fork.

Fine crystal the likes of which Victoria had never seen before graced the table alongside gold-banded white china bearing the hotel's insignia. Victoria wondered if she would ever learn the uses of the various stemmed goblets and tiny dishes.

Dark-skinned waiters, neatly uniformed in black suits and white gloves, hovered everywhere, ready to remove each course at the moment of its completion and bring out the next, all without the slightest clinking of flatware against porcelain. Muffled conversations filled an atmosphere rich with the appealing bouquet of delicate seasonings.

The meal seemed never-ending, with its long list of offerings. Soups, fish, relishes, boiled and roast meats, entrees, salads, vegetables, pastry, and desserts all appeared in due course, and at the very end, coffee or tea.

Never had Victoria seen or been served so much food! She regretted having indulged so heartily in the main course when she tasted the utter richness of the dessert of blueberries and cream.

But she would likely never return here after tomorrow evening, so Lily was right. She might as well enjoy herself.

Lily's Aunt Agatha seemed to approve of Victoria. The crusty old widow accompanied the young girls on a stroll down the 627-foot porch, then took to a rocker while Lily and Victoria walked its length once more. The elderly woman kept such a sharp eye on her charges, Victoria could nearly feel her gaze burning into her back.

Lily returned the greeting of a tall blond fellow, then commented to Victoria, "Don't mind Auntie's watchfulness, Tory, and for goodness sake, keep smiling."

The young Manhattan debutante continued toward the east end of the veranda, nodding to a dapper gentleman of about forty, unmindful that the handsome young man with the fair hair was taking a particularly close look at her.

When the evening sky finally darkened, they climbed the grand staircase to the second floor once again, Aunt Agatha with a steadying hand in the crook of Lily's elbow. She was a gracious, caring companion to the elderly woman, attentive to her every comfort and respectful with her every word.

"Aren't you ready yet? It's nearly noon."

Victoria had opened the door to Lily's knock, and now stood before the mirror to secure loose pins in her chestnut hair. She had just returned from a trip to the telegraph office on Main Street where she had sent a message to her father.

BUSINESS NOT CONCLUDED. RETURN DELAYED. WILL ADVISE. LOVE, VICTORIA.

"There. I'm all set." She shoved the last hairpin into place and reached for her unadorned straw hat.

Before she could pick it up, Lily snatched the hat away and studied it. Then her eyes swept over Victoria from head to toe, bringing a disapproving cluck of the tongue.

Victoria had donned the pinstripe suit this morning, with a plain white waist. Still clutching the hat, Lily crossed quickly to the closet. Taking a ruffled shirtwaist from the rod, she thrust it into Victoria's hands.

"Here. Put this on."

"I'm going for a business meeting, not a social outing," Victoria protested.

"That's what *you* think. You've got to create the right impression.

Now trust me. I'll be right back." In a trice, she was gone.

Reluctantly, Victoria accepted Lily's advice. Before she had finished buttoning the last lacy cuff, the girl had returned.

Victoria's plain straw hat now sported a wide pink silk bow about the crown. In Lily's hand was an even wider matching scarf. She set the hat on the dresser and drew the scarf about Victoria's neck, tying it into a floppy bow. Victoria adjusted the hat on her head, securing it with a long, gold-headed hat pin.

Lily studied the effect of her adornments. "A slight improvement, but only slight," she concluded.

"You needn't have gone to all this fuss and bother, Lily."

"Oh, stuff! It was no bother." Lily handed Victoria the gloves and parasol she had left laying on her bed. "Now off with you. It's noon. Your carriage awaits."

Victoria slid her portfolio under her arm and locked the door behind her. "Thanks, Lily. See you later!"

"Don't forget to have a good time, Tory!"

Victoria was halfway to the staircase when she heard Lily use the dreaded nickname. Too late to scold her now. She turned and waved. *A good time? Nonsense!* For her, this was business, no matter what Lily had said.

At the porte cochère Big John handed her into an elegant, open *vis-à-vis* identified with the hotel badge. She rested against the tufted velvet seat back, unfolded her parasol, and inhaled the fresh-water air blowing in off the straits, a cooling breeze against the warmth of the sun, which blazed down from a brilliant blue, cloudless sky.

A short drive brought them to a rise in a clearing where a wooden observatory had been built, consisting of two flights of stairs leading to an elevated platform where a half-dozen tourists were enjoying the view. She was surprised to see that a table with an umbrella had been erected near the observatory, and that Rand Bartlett stood in conversation with a waiter.

He quickly extracted himself when Victoria's carriage rolled into sight. As he crossed the clearing, he chuckled to himself at the persistence she had shown yesterday. He had never come up against a young woman with such a natural, unaffected dignity. It was quite disarming!

Most of the young ladies who came to Grand Hotel as guests were simpering, pampered daughters of the newly rich, indulged to excess by parents who had found yet another way to spend their recently acquired wealth.

Victoria Whitmore was obviously no pampered hothouse flower, but something of a hollyhock, possessing a strong, straight spine in a garden of drooping pansies. And the bee that had worked her blossoms had somehow dusted him with her pollen, and the magic granules had worked their way into his system, giving him a desire to keep her on the island for at least today.

Being controlled by thoughts of a woman wasn't like Rand at all. He had taken such a cavalier attitude toward the fairer sex most of his thirty-five years. The less reputable of them were a convenience when the urge arose to satisfy his manly desires. Those of loftier morals provided an entree into exclusive social circles. But he had always been in complete control, even when pursued by beautiful, wealthy debutantes in full bloom and begging to be picked.

Always, *except* ... his thoughts drifted back. There was a time, a summer here on the island ... he had tried to erase the memory from his mind, but every so often it crept back in, reminding him he had once been in love. The romance had ended so unexpectedly, so painfully, he had vowed never to love again.

Until Miss Whitmore had come along he had been in no danger of breaking that vow.

Miss Victoria Whitmore was another matter indeed. He offered her an engaging smile, taking her hand as she alighted from the *vis-à-vis*. And he tried to warn himself against getting too close.

"Welcome, Miss Whitmore. How stunning you look, with those dashes of pink bringing out the roses in your cheeks."

Victoria's color deepened. She was unaccustomed to being the recipient of such a compliment, and replied perfunctorily, "Thank you, Mr. Bartlett. Quite a luncheon you have planned, I see." She referred to the elegantly set table spread with fine linen and laden with the same exquisite china, crystal and silver she had eaten from in the hotel dining room. Nearby, a picnic hamper stood open on a rack while the waiter prepared to serve the meal.

"Nothing is too good for a guest of Rand Bartlett."

To Victoria, the remark sounded more self-serving than complimentary. "Nothing except paying me my due. Isn't that right, Mr. Bartlett?"

"Please, Miss Whitmore. Discussion of such a topic will go so much more smoothly on a full stomach. Let's agree to drop the matter until later."

"I get the feeling that with you, Mr. Bartlett, later may never come."

He laughed openly with amusement. "Then I give you my word I will not let the day pass without settling the matter to which you refer." He took the portfolio from beneath her arm and tossed it onto the carriage seat. "For now, let's forget business." Tucking Victoria's hand in the crook of his elbow, he led her toward the observation tower, pausing to pick up a pair of field glasses from the table. "Did you sleep well?"

"Would *you*, knowing the difference between carrying on in business and being forced to close up shop may well rest in your ability to convince a single creditor to come through with a payment he has owed for the past three months?"

"I thought we had agreed to set the matter aside."

"*You* had."

"Then what will it take for me to convince you?"

"A check for what you owe would be sufficient. I'm certain I could enjoy your picnic very much, were I to acquire that."

"I give you my word. The matter will be settled to your satisfaction yet today."

"Your contract called for payment three months ago, yet after several billings, I have received nothing. What reason have I to trust your word?"

His broad smile never faded. "None. None whatever. But I'm not about to produce a check from up my sleeve like some prestidigitator, so you will have to exercise patience for the time being, Miss Whitmore. Do you think you can manage that long enough to enjoy the view?"

"Perhaps, but don't test me. I didn't come for the hospitality or the food. I'll get what I'm after."

"Of that, I have no doubt." His hand at her elbow, he assisted her up the stairs to the platform.

When they had reached the top of the tower, he offered her the field glasses, and her thoughts were soon engulfed by the vision before her of islands and water and peninsulas.

She could pick out Fort Mackinac, the village below it and the docks,

even the mainland. About the island were fabulous limestone forma-
tions, giving way to the ribbon of water called the straits, shimmering
and rippling along a path between Lakes Michigan and Huron.

"This view is breathtaking," she said in wonderment. For a moment
she was almost glad Grand Hotel hadn't paid its bill. Otherwise, she
would never have left Grand Rapids, never have peeked into this world
so foreign to her--this fresh, clean wonderland filled with unspeakable
beauty.

"I thought you'd enjoy it," Rand replied, obviously pleased. "After
luncheon, I'll take you to some of the most interesting sites."

A few minutes later, Victoria was seated across from Rand at the
round table and the waiter set to work.

The affair lacked nothing of the accoutrements of formal dining.
Young chickens fried to perfection, fresh fruit salad, and chocolate layer
cake made it the finest luncheon Victoria had ever tasted. She had to
suppress a laugh when she mentally compared it to the egg sandwiches
she and her parents had taken along on their picnics beside the Grand
River in years gone by.

Conversation remained pleasant and impersonal, and by the time the
last of the chocolate cake had disappeared, Rand had convinced Victoria
that in all of Michigan, no finer climate could be found than that on
Mackinac Island. "Why, even William Cullen Bryant predicted in 1846
that the island would become a summer gathering place."

"And his prophecy has been fulfilled," Victoria concluded.

"So it has. Now, if you're willing, I'd like to show you some of the
natural attractions of the island, and perhaps we can come to terms
regarding business matters."

"I'd be delighted to discuss the matter you've been avoiding since my
arrival on the island."

When they had settled in the carriage, she lifted her portfolio from the
back seat where he had tossed it earlier, and opened it on her lap.

Rand gave directions to Big John, then adjusted the brim of his straw
hat against the bright sun.

Victoria handed him her copy of the original billing and the two
statements she had sent over the last three months, half expecting him to
again shove them aside. Instead, he scrutinized each document before
raising his warm hazel eyes to meet her clear, gray ones.

"I'm certain I've seen these on my desk," he admitted in all serious-ness. "In fact, I remember signing this," he held up the most recent statement, "and directing Hubert ... Hubert Munson, my accountant ... to pay it in full, but he didn't seem to remember it when I asked him about it yesterday afternoon.

"He's new to my employ, but he's been very reliable in the short time he's been with me. I remember that quite a stack of paperwork was left for him by the previous hotel administration and it's always possible it got lost in the shuffle.

"I'll give this to him the moment we return to the hotel, and have him send the check up to your room yet this afternoon." He handed back the other two papers then folded the most recent statement and slipped it into the inside pocket of his seersucker suit. "Will that satisfy you, Miss Whitmore?"

She tucked the papers into her portfolio. "This afternoon will be fine, Mr. Bartlett." Relieved at his promise, she laid her leather folder aside and reached for her parasol before realizing the driver had turned onto a shady trail.

The cool, dim forest lane offered a welcome canopy against the soar-ing afternoon temperature. Though Victoria had tried to remain cool and calm, beads of moisture began to dot her upper lip before she managed to blot it with her handkerchief.

Across from her, Rand relaxed fully against his seat back, extending his legs. The brush of his knee against her dress awoke disturbing sensa-tions inside her. She adjusted her position, drawing away from him as much as possible in the cramped space. Glancing up from beneath her crisp straw hat brim, she detected a look of thoughtful menace in the curl of his lip. Nervously, she checked the time on her lapel watch, trying to ignore the broadening grin on the handsome face across from her.

"Perhaps there will be more to your venture here on the island than just collecting on my account. I would hate to see you return to Grand Rapids until you've had an opportunity to properly enjoy all the island has to offer. It would be nice if you could look back favorably on your stay at Grand Hotel."

"Perhaps someday I will." Victoria would concede nothing, still resenting the difficulties he had put her through. He did seem to be trying to make it up to her in his own way, though. She must try to ignore the discomfiture his close presence offered and concentrate on the pleasant ride.

The island's wooded interior seemed peaceful compared with the crowded shoreline, bustling village, and busy hotel lobby. High above, the trill of a warbler sang descant to the muffled clatter of the *vis-à-vis*, and the perfume of the pines offered a soothing balm. In spite of Rand's sprawling legs, Victoria consciously willed herself to relax into the sumptuous diamond tufting of her seat, though it meant brushing the hem of her skirt against his pant leg. She even took off her gloves and laid them aside.

Rounding a curve, the driver pulled off into a small clearing where a large rock jutted sharply toward the bright sun.

"Lover's Leap. That's what they call it. Are you familiar with the legend, Miss Whitmore?" She barely had shaken her head in response when he sprang from the carriage. "Walk with me while I tell you the tale."

She reached for her parasol and was considering whether to again pull on her gloves, but decided against it. A few tourists were strolling nearby, but certainly no one familiar to her who would be shocked to see her gloveless.

She prepared to step down from the carriage, but instead, Rand caught her about the waist with two strong hands and lifted her to the ground. The unexpected contact did strange, forbidden things to her pulse.

"You needn't have been so exuberant in your assistance, Mr. Bartlett," she chided. "I'm not a small child."

"You can be certain I've taken note of *that*, Miss Whitmore." He guided her away from the carriage and driver with his hand at the small of her back.

Flustered, she quickly popped open her parasol, but it failed to catch, and collapsed around her head. The difficulty brought a warm chuckle from her escort, and a helping hand.

"Allow me, Miss Whitmore." Spreading the parasol once more, he held it between them, placing her hand in the crook of his arm and resting his own over it.

Victoria felt utterly naked with her bare hand beneath his, the texture of his seersucker jacket against her palm. She hadn't anticipated such intimacy when deciding to leave her gloves behind. Yet for some unknown reason, she didn't protest.

"As you were saying, Mr. Bartlett, the rock is called Lover's Leap?"

He guided Victoria on a path around the perimeter of the clearing, speaking softly, as if the tale were somehow sacred. "The name comes from an old Ojibway legend about a young Indian maiden, *Lo-tah*. Her lover went off to war against the Iroquois to prove himself a man fit enough to marry a chief's daughter."

"And did her lover return to find she had taken up with another, and spurned, fling himself from the top?" Victoria quietly asked.

"No, he didn't. *Lo-tah* climbed the rock each day to await his return. Many months later, when the Ojibway warriors came home, she learned that *Ge-niw-e-gwon* had been killed. Every day for the next seven days, *Lo-tah* dreamed of a beautiful bird, the spirit of her lover, visiting her atop the high rock. On the eighth day, when her father came to see her, he found her crumpled body at the bottom of the precipice."

"So it was *Lo-tah* who threw herself off."

Rand nodded. "To enter the spirit world and be forever joined with her lover. Since that time, this rock has been known as Lover's Leap." His smooth, soft voice could almost lull Victoria into a trance, but she resisted his allure.

In spite of his attractive qualities, she was determined not to be taken in. She wondered, after all, how many other women he had escorted to this very spot to hear him relate the tale of Lover's Leap in a seductive timbre.

"A very interesting legend, Mr. Bartlett," she said quite matter-of-factly. "Thank you for sharing it with me. I'll remember it whenever I think back on this trip. Now, if you'll be so kind as to escort me back to the hotel?"

"Of course. I'll have John drive us back directly."

She reached for her parasol, and thought in spite of Rand's agreeable words, he gave it over reluctantly.

In the carriage, Victoria fussed with her gloves, her portfolio, the arrangement of her skirt, and sat perfectly rigid on the edge of her seat, determined to maintain proper deportment.

She could sense Rand's gaze on her and ventured a fleeting glance his way, only to discover a look of undisguised amusement. Feigning interest in the scenery, she turned abruptly away, irritated at finding herself the source of his pleasure.

At the porte cochère, he helped her down from the *vis-à-vis* in a correct, dignified manner and walked her inside.

"Thank you, Mr. Bartlett, for the delightful outing, and even more so for your promise of payment. I'll expect your check yet today."

He withdrew the billing from his breast pocket and tapped it across his palm. "I'm on my way to see Munson about it this very minute. Good day, Miss Whitmore." In a flash, he had melted into the group of guests milling about the lobby.

Victoria couldn't help thinking, as she climbed the grand staircase to her second floor room, how his personality had seemed to change from relaxed, amused escort to efficient manager the moment he stepped back inside Grand Hotel. Such was the requirement of his position, she reckoned.

She hadn't been in her room more than a few seconds when Lily peered around the door. "Tory, you're back!" She sounded gleeful, as if her only friend had returned from a 'round the world cruise. "I've been wondering for the longest time what happened." The door had been left ajar, but Lily closed it behind her now.

"Lily, come in," Victoria said wryly. "I can tell you in one sentence what happened. He promised to send a check up to me this afternoon. And Lily, please don't call me Tory."

"But the afternoon is nearly over, *Victoria*. Where have you been all this time? Why didn't he give you the payment? Is this another stall?"

Chapter 3

Victoria dissolved in laughter. It was that, or become angry all over again that she had let Bartlett slip away scot-free, and she'd had enough of that already.

"Tory Whitmore--Victoria, I mean--you're impossible," Lily scolded petulantly, then collapsed into giggles herself.

When Victoria regained her composure, she put her arm about her newfound friend's shoulders and walked her toward the door. "I suppose you'd like to hear chapter and verse of the afternoon's events, but to tell you the truth, I need some time to myself. It's been quite a day, and I'd like to rest until dinner. By the way, Mr. Bartlett complimented your pink scarf. Now out with you."

"Auntie and I will stop by for you on our way down to dinner at six."

"I'll see you then." Victoria closed the door behind Lily.

Alone, Victoria thought back on her outing with Rand. If he had been trying to impress her with his picnic, he had certainly succeeded. To think he had gone to so much trouble to arrange an outing--a much simpler luncheon would have sufficed, spread on a blanket beneath a shade tree. The memory of being served formally in the out-of-doors would remain with her for some time.

The afternoon had passed in a most pleasant fashion, a fact she was loath to admit even to herself. She felt a certain attraction to the hotel manager: the hazel eyes so full of life, the lock of hair that fell over his forehead, the strong line of his cheekbone. His features, combined with his gentle, refined manner created an undeniable appeal.

Now, if he would only pay her, she thought. Taking a clothes brush from her bag, she set to work ridding the hem of her skirt of dust.

She had completed the task and was straightening her few belongings on her dresser top when a knock sounded on her door. Certain Rand's check had arrived by bellboy, she hurried to answer.

Robert, the young man who had introduced her to Rand's assistant the day before, stood in the hallway.

"Mr. Bartlett asked me to bring you this message and wait for the favor of your response."

Victoria noted her name written in tiny script across the envelope's face. "Of course, Robert. If you'll excuse me a moment?" She stepped into her room and pried open the flap, expecting to find a check and a receipt requiring her signature as proof she had received the payment. Her hands trembled as she unfolded the paper, thinking how good it would be to finally have possession of the large sum owed. But there was no check inside. The message, written in a neat hand, read:

> Victoria,
>
> Munson left work early this afternoon. Please accept my sincere apology for delay of payment and let me make it up to you by escorting you to this evening's dance on the front lawn.
>
> Can you meet me at nine in the foyer? I'll be busy with preparations until that time. Please give Robert your response in the affirmative.
>
> Most humbly, RB

Seething, Victoria ripped Rand Bartlett's note into tiny pieces, poured it back into the envelope, and strode to her door, bumping headlong into Lily. The bits of paper flew from the envelope and scattered like confetti across the floor.

"Tory! I'm sorry, I didn't mean to ..." She scooped up a handful of the shredded paper. "What's this? A celebration? Your check came!"

"Check? Before, I doubted that Mr. Rand Bartlett knew the meaning of the word. Now, I'm *certain* he doesn't." She sputtered indignantly. "He says his accountant left work early and he won't be able to pay me today. Then, he had the effrontery to invite me to be his guest at the dance tonight, as if that could make up for it."

"You're going, aren't you?" Lily asked innocently.

"I most certainly am not." She stepped outside the door, forcing herself to reply calmly to Robert. "You can tell Mr. Bartlett my answer is no."

"Yes, ma'am."

The bellboy turned to leave, but Lily stayed him with a hand on his sleeve. "No, Robert. Wait." She pleaded with Victoria. "You've *got* to go. Can't you see? A refusal will only make things worse. Besides, what plans have you for the evening? At least three dozen eligible young ladies staying in this hotel would give anything to be in your place tonight." She turned to Robert. "Tell him yes. The answer is yes. Miss Whitmore will be honored to be Mr. Bartlett's guest."

"Lily, you're interfering. I'm not going," Victoria stated, undeterred. She addressed Robert with equal determination. "You can tell Mr. Bartlett I decline." She whirled away, stepping into her room and closing the door. A few seconds later, Lily entered.

"Tory, *please* listen to me." She went to the dresser and opened the top drawer, extracting a piece of hotel stationery. Uncapping the fountain pen Victoria had left out, she began writing furiously. "Just send him a little acceptance. What will it hurt? You'll be so much better off. Now, if you'll just sign this ..." She handed Victoria the pen and paper.

Victoria hesitated, then decided it couldn't hurt to read Lily's message.

> RB,
>
>   How kind of you to invite me as your guest for this evening's entertainment. I shall be looking for you in the foyer at nine.
> Appreciatively,

Reading Lily's words had a calming effect. A tiny part of Victoria wished the two polite sentences were true. But they were far from it. She shook her head, chuckling out loud at the preposterous thought. "It will never work, Lily. Even if I wanted to go, which I don't, I have nothing to wear. You said yourself my wardrobe is lacking. Besides, I don't even know how to dance."

"Oh, hush! I can fix up your wardrobe. And if you'll come with me to the parlor, there's a dancing lesson going on this very minute. No excuses, Tory! This is for your own good. Can't you see?"

Victoria stared down into her friend's round face. Something about the glint in Lily's clear blue eyes, and the determined look which forced her brows together into a "v" made Victoria want to throw her hands in the air.

"All right. If it will please you, Lily, I'll go to the parlor for lessons, and I'll go to the dance. I'll even let you fix up my wardrobe. But I won't enjoy it. Not one little bit." She penned a hasty "V. Whitmore" on the bottom of Lily's note.

Triumphantly, Lily folded the paper and tucked it into a matching hotel envelope. "You'll thank me, Tory. You'll see the good of it, I promise."

Lily's hand was on the door when Victoria called out, "Aren't you forgetting something? Robert is already on his way to Mr. Bartlett with my refusal. Unless you're planning to deliver that note yourself, it will never reach him. Even if it did, he'd never believe it after my first response."

A mischievous gleam in her eye, she replied, "You want to bet?" Flinging open the door, she revealed a patient Robert waiting in the hallway. Lily pressed the acceptance into the bellboy's hand, along with something from her pocket. A tip, Victoria assumed, and likely a generous one at that. "To Mr. Bartlett, posthaste!" Lily directed.

"Yes, miss. Thank you, miss." With a deferential bow, he was gone.

Lily eyed her friend. "Now, we're off to the parlor, before Mr. Cachetti concludes his lesson for the day."

At the parlor door, Lily had to practically force Victoria to cross the threshhold of the elegant room. Brocaded couches, velvet straight-backed chairs, and wicker rockers were arranged in casual groups at the near end. At the opposite end of the room stood an open grate with a lavishly tiled mantelpiece and hearth, and in front of this, the Turkey carpet had been rolled back. In the air, Victoria detected the faintest hint of lemon oil polish, which had given the oak woodwork a warm glow.

Chopin's *Minute Waltz* issued forth from a spinet piano, and couples moved smoothly in time to the rhythm. Victoria fidgeted with the bow beneath her chin, feeling an overwhelming urge to leave before anyone noticed her.

With a firm hand on Victoria's elbow, Lily started across the room. "Don't be so nervous. No one here is going to bite you," she teased.

"They might when they see how awkward I am! Oh, Lily, let's forget it. I'll tell Mr. Bartlett I don't care to dance. He doesn't have to know that I never learned how!" Victoria turned to go.

"Nonsense!" In a stern whisper, she scolded, "You can't leave now. Mr. Cachetti will be offended." The dance instructor, clad in a silk Italian suit, was crossing the bare floor to greet them. "Besides," she quietly added, "with your height, you're more elegant than even the most graceful debutante from my class. You'll master the waltz in no time."

Elegant. It was the first time anyone had described her so. Victoria had always perceived herself as gangly, with too-long arms and legs. Perhaps a lesson wouldn't be so awful.

When Lily introduced Victoria to the suave dance master, he kissed her hand in a manner laden with old-world charm, then brought her to the center of the floor to take her through the simple waltz steps. *One*-two-three, *one*-two-three. Stiff at first, Victoria was soon caught up with the infectious rhythm of Chopin. In moments they were circling about the room.

"Excellent. Excellent, my dear," Cachetti encouraged, "So quickly, you learn."

Victoria had begun to relax into the pattern. Across the room she caught sight of Lily on the arm of Mr. Donovan. Though Victoria couldn't say why, something about Rand Bartlett's assistant made her feel uneasy. When she nearly missed a step, she renewed her concentration on the waltz. Around and around the parlor she went, feeling light as the summer air.

By the time Mr. Cachetti had concluded his dance lesson, Victoria had gained enough confidence in herself to attend the evening dance with Rand Bartlett. Returning to the second floor, she freshened herself in the washroom, then crossed the hall to her room to pondered the meager selection of clothing hanging in her closet. Lily found her there when she entered with white lace dripping from one of her arms, a hat and sewing box cradled in the other.

"Miss Atwood's Alterations at your service. Too bad we're not the same height, Tory. I have a whole closet full of things that would be just right for this evening, if we were."

"I've asked myself a thousand times why I had to grow so tall. It's a problem, finding anything the proper length," Victoria admitted. She fingered the lacy fabric of the shawl Lily carried. It was far more delicate than any she had ever owned. "Oh, Lily, this is beautiful, much too fine for me."

"Not according to Aunt Agatha, and we both know Aunt Agatha is *always* right. Now, let's see ..." She sauntered to the closet. Brows wrinkling over her nose, she withdrew the plain shirtwaist she had rejected for Victoria earlier that day and laid it out on the bed. Opening her sewing box, she removed needle and thread, and a filigree lace collarette. "Here. While you're tacking this over your plain collar, I'll start on the cuffs."

She rummaged again in her sewing box, withdrawing a length of white braid embroidered with lavender satin roses, and began stitching it in place.

A few minutes later, she snipped her thread with a tiny pair of gold sewing scissors and inspected the decorated cuffs. "There. It's a new creation."

Victoria tied a knot and cut her thread, then held the shirtwaist up against her small bosom and strolled to the mirror above her dresser. The lacy collarette softened the line of her cheekbones, and the braid-trimmed cuffs added femininity to her long arms. She slipped the waist on over her chemise and buttoned it, turning this way and that to admire its effect on her plain skirt. "How can I thank you, Lily?"

"You needn't thank me. Actually, most of this is from Aunt Agatha. In fact, right here in her box is a pretty little silk rose for your shirtwaist. It matches the ones on your cuffs, and those on the brim of Auntie's hat." She pinned on the lavender rose, centering it between the points of the added lace collarette. "And don't forget to take the shawl to keep the cool night air off your shoulders."

Victoria tried on the filmy white lace, admiring its drape over her arms. Carefully, she removed the cover, folded it and handed it to Lily. "I couldn't possibly wear this. It's much too delicate."

"Auntie specifically told me to bring it to you. I'll *not* return it to her." She checked Victoria's watch. "It's nearly dinner time. You're dining with us this evening, aren't you?"

"Yes, that would be lovely, thank you."

"I'm going to get Auntie now. You can come with me and return the shawl if you wish, but I would suggest you swallow that pride of yours and just thank her. She doesn't take kindly to those who turn away her generosity."

Victoria paused to consider Lily's suggestion. "I'm truly grateful to you both for helping me. You're spoiling me, you know."

Lily laughed. "Not a chance," she countered, then hurried out the door.

By the time Victoria sat down to dinner with Lily and Agatha, the apprehension building in her over the dance had set a swarm of gnats loose in her stomach. She tried to put her queasiness from her mind, but with little success.

"You needn't trouble yourself over the engagement," Agatha advised her. "Any man who doesn't favor you over those brainless, witless creatures that seem to abound hereabouts, simply isn't worth your concern."

Victoria felt the warmth of embarrassment coloring her cheeks. "You flatter me, Mrs. Atwood."

"I speak the truth. You're worthy of the attention of any man I've seen yet on this island, but I've seen plenty who aren't worth your time. As for this Bartlett fellow, I think there's something to him. He just might be worth your trouble."

"I'm thankful for your opinion, Mrs. Atwood. I'll admit I haven't much experience where men are concerned. By the time I was thirteen, I'd already grown to my present height and was taller than most of the fellows my own age. Naturally, they paid me little attention. Besides, I've been too busy helping Papa to give thought to social outings. I'm ashamed to admit this will be my first dance."

Agatha waved aside the young woman's concern. "You'll do fine. Just stay light on your toes and let the gentleman lead, no matter how clumsy he might be. And remember what Benjamin Franklin said. 'When you speak to a man, look on his eyes. When he speaks to you, look on his mouth.'"

Victoria smiled politely. "I'll remember."

It was well past eight o'clock by the time Victoria had returned from dinner, and Lily joined her in her room. "Now, Victoria, have a wonderful time. Don't even bother to think about me all alone with Auntie, tucked away on the second floor for the entire evening." Her expression drew into an exaggerated pout.

Victoria chuckled nervously at her friend's attempt to humor her. "I wish you were going to this dance instead of me, or at the very least, were going to be there, too. You've had so much practice at this sort of thing, having formally 'come out' and all. What's it like to be a debutante, anyway?"

"Not as grand as you might think, Tory. Be glad you didn't have to go through it--each girl trying to outdo the other--or, rather, the mothers are."

Victoria stood before her mirror checking her appearance one last time. "I thought it would have been fun, having all those new gowns made." She removed a pin from her French twist, fidgeted with a strand of hair, and shoved the pin back in place.

"Tory, will you stop your fussing? You're even beginning to make *me* nervous." Lily cast a knowing smile at her friend. "Mr. Bartlett really has made quite an impression on you, hasn't he?"

Victoria turned from the mirror, an accusing look in her blue-gray eyes. "How would you know?"

"It's true, isn't it?" Lily allowed an awkward moment of silence to pass, then smiled engagingly. "You needn't admit it, and you needn't worry. For once I agree with Auntie. Just be yourself, Tory. If that's not good enough for Mr. Bartlett, then you're better off not seeing him. *Except* to get your payment, that is."

Victoria sighed. "The payment. If not for that, I wouldn't trouble myself." She fussed at the silk rose on her waist.

"I think you would." She started for the door. "I'd better go check on Auntie and leave you to collect your thoughts. The big hour is only minutes away." She impulsively hugged Victoria, then let herself out.

For the tenth time, Victoria checked her white gloves to see that they were spotless. "I don't know why I bother looking. I haven't any other clean pair," she mumbled to herself. Key in hand, she let herself out and locked the door. Taking a deep breath, she squared her shoulders, tried to assume a natural smile, and attempted to calm herself by strolling leisurely down the hall. Nevertheless, her runaway heartbeat refused to slow its frantic pace.

As she descended the grand staircase, Victoria imagined herself, for the briefest moment, to be a wealthy debutante about to make her debut into society. She was no longer the daughter of an impoverished woodcarver, but a desirable young lady. Holding herself in a regal manner, she paused slightly on each step, smiling down at the waiting guests. It mattered not that she wore a plain navy blue skirt and an even plainer blouse that owed its decorative trim to a generous friend. Only Lily and Agatha knew that the exquisite lace shawl dripping from her elbows did not belong to her. This was her long-awaited hour, her first dance.

Then, her eyes met Rand's and reality charged in where dreams had dared to tread. Her gallant escort, who awaited her arrival at the bottom of the stairs, grinned up at her with that lopsided, impish expression of his.

Had he read her silly thoughts?

Victoria's pulse fluttered wildly and an intense warmth rushed through her, coloring her cheeks no less than crimson, she was certain. Suddenly, she felt like Cinderella at the *end* of the ball, and wanted to scurry away like the mice who had pulled the pumpkin carriage.

But there was no escape. Her dread of this engagement quickly returned double-strength, yet she must make the best of it for Papa's sake, and her own. She inhaled deeply and tried to relax the facial muscles that had gone stiff with panic.

"Miss Victoria, you're looking quite charming this evening. I'm convinced you should always wear roses. They become you so." Only the unmistakable sincerity in his tone prevented Victoria's blush from deepening.

"Thank you, Mr. Bartlett." She looked up into his twinkling hazel eyes, then allowed her gaze to take in the rest of him. He wore a light gray suit, a white silk shirt with studded buttons, and a neat bow tie, all tailored to enhance his solid physique, and it had its effect on her. Disappointed as she was over his delay of payment, she couldn't deny she felt drawn to him.

Placing Victoria's hand on his arm, Rand continued, "Now that I think of it, there is a rose called 'Victoria,' isn't there? A particularly large and fragrant blossom prized among gardeners?"

"Are you sure you don't mean the cabbage rose?"

Rand chuckled lightly. "Oh, no. I'm fairly certain it's the 'Victoria,' or, if not, it should be."

They exited the grand portico. "If there is such a variety, it must have been named for the queen," Victoria concluded.

Rand laughed openly. "For that dour woman? Heaven forbid. A rose should be named for a woman of beauty and femininity, of grace and charm."

Victoria quickly looked away. *Does he consider me so?* she wondered as they descended the many stairs to the lawn and strolled among the roses, their sweet fragrance permeating the dusky air. Colored lanterns strung about the perimeter of the garden glowed festively, and the melodic strains lilting from violin bows lured them into the three-quarter rhythm of the waltz.

"Shall we?" Rand assisted her onto the dance platform and assumed the stance of a proper waltz partner, placing his right hand ever so lightly against Victoria's back.

She stepped off with him to the music, gliding, gliding, *one*-two-three, *one*-two-three. He moved as smoothly as the dance instructor had, taking her with him, making her forget the awkwardness she usually felt because of her height. He stood perhaps only two inches taller than she, but he danced as though he were born to it.

How elegant he made her feel, how confident and carefree. Only minutes before she had dreaded this time with him; now she found herself wishing the evening would never end.

"I do wish you were staying past tomorrow," Rand commented. "I'm planning the biggest event ever for the hotel--for the whole island, in fact--this coming weekend."

"How perfectly modest of you to say so," Victoria accused, offering him a teasing smile. "I really should be on my way to Grand Rapids even now, and would have been, if it weren't for your wayward accountant."

"You've set your mind on going as soon as you receive payment, and I can't persuade you to stay?"

Though the turn of conversation had taken Victoria by surprise, she somehow managed to follow Rand's lead without missing a step. She could dream that he had mentioned her staying on because he cared about her, and deep in her heart she wished it were so, but she was no fool. He was a shrewd hotel manager looking to fill every room, she reminded herself, and he would likely tap every means to accomplish his goal. "I'll be on my way to the ferry dock the moment I have your payment in hand, Mr. Bartlett."

"That's your prerogative, I suppose." He pulled her closer and circled wide around the dance floor, nearly sweeping Victoria off her feet at times.

For the next two dances, Rand said little, guiding Victoria on winged feet about the wooden platform. Though couples moved past them to the measured time, they seemed almost of another world, and Victoria felt transported to some magic isle where only she and Rand existed. For this one evening she was a princess; he, her fairy-tale prince. For now she would put out of her mind any ulterior motives he might have had in trying to entice her to stay on Mackinac.

The third waltz had ended when Mr. Donovan approached him. "Excuse me, Mr. Bartlett. I'm sorry to interrupt, but I must have a word with you."

"I'll only be a minute," Rand assured her, then reluctantly followed Donovan away from the crowd of dancers.

Donovan seemed impatient, gesturing toward the hotel as he led Bartlett off the wooden platform.

Victoria's fragile dream world had cracked, and once again reality came crashing in. Her heart sank as she watched the two men ascend the stairs, cross the drive beneath the porte cochère and disappear inside the hotel.

The orchestra struck up a two step, and she felt as conspicuous as an ugly duckling on a lake afloat with white swans. Eyes downcast, she made her way from the dance floor, wondering where she could go to await Rand's return without feeling out of place. The dim shadows fringing the garden seemed most appealing. She stepped off in that direction, turning her back to the hotel and dance platform.

Below Cadotte Avenue, the boarding houses and hotels sent hazy yellow lights into the murky darkness. Beyond them, Haldimand Bay and the straits remained calm.

Tomorrow, she would collect her check, and in the bright sunshine of midmorning, board the ferry, homewardbound. Though she hadn't wanted to leave Grand Rapids, she now realized a part of her was in no hurry to return.

She was silently arguing against these irrational feelings when a hand cupped her elbow. She turned to face Donovan, her heart flooding with disappointment.

"Mr. Bartlett must attend to some urgent business. He asked me to extend his deepest apologies. It would be my pleasure to accompany you on the dance floor." His words were kind and gentle, not clipped as they had been on their first meeting.

Victoria's heart sank below her knees, but she managed to force the corners of her mouth upward. "You needn't feel obligated, Mr. Donovan. If you'll just see me to my room--"

"Obligated? Privileged would be more accurate, Miss Whitmore. Shall we waltz?" He offered his arm.

Victoria searched his shadowed expression for some hint of insincerity, but found instead the steady gaze of admiring brown eyes. Across his cheekbones was a spattering of freckles she hadn't noticed before, and they gave him a charming, innocent appeal. She placed her hand on his arm.

They mounted the dance platform and stepped in time to the music. Donovan was a skilled dancer, rivaling Rand Bartlett for smoothness and grace.

He seemed to have mastered the art of small talk, too. For some time they exchanged pleasantries about the island and Grand Hotel, avoiding anything of a personal nature.

When the orchestra took a break, he settled her into a chair. She removed her gloves and stuffed them into her handbag while he went for punch and cookies. She glanced furtively in the direction of the hotel door from time to time, hoping to see Rand Bartlett return, but the last waltz found her still in Donovan's arms, being held much closer than she would have liked.

When the dance ended, he linked her arm with his and walked her toward the hotel. "Mr. Bartlett's business must have kept him longer than he expected. I'll be happy to see you to your room, Miss Whitmore."

"You needn't go to such trouble, Mr. Donovan."

"Why, it's no trouble at all. In fact, I insist." His hand at her back, he guided her inside the front door and up the staircase.

As they neared her room, she removed her key from her handbag. "If you'll give Mr. Bartlett a message for me, I'd be most appreciative. Please tell him I'll come by his office tomorrow morning at half past eight to settle our business matter."

They had stopped outside her door, and Donovan took the key from her and unlocked her room. The gesture made Victoria uneasy, as if he were about to intrude on her privacy.

"I'll certainly pass the information along. Now, I'll bid you good night, and pleasant dreams." He took her bare hand in his and kissed her palm. Then he pressed her key into it, folding her fingers around it. He stood there a moment, holding her hand in both of his and looking deep into her eyes, as if trying to read some message there.

Victoria withdrew from his disconcerting touch and cleared her throat. "Well, then. Good night, Mr. Donovan, and thank you." She stepped inside her room and closed the door, sending home the bolt and fastening the chain.

Leaning her back against the door, she let out a sigh. Though she was inexperienced with men, she had no difficulty recognizing that Mr. Donovan was more attracted to her than she was to him despite his many good qualities--his agility on the dance floor, his expertise in conversation, his attentiveness.

The look he had given her before departing still made her feel uneasy. A most distressing possibility crossed her mind. Suppose he had thought she was one of "those" girls?

"Good heavens to Betsy," she muttered. But it made sense. Here she was, 250 miles from home, unattached, and traveling without a chaperone.

She nearly laughed aloud. "Well, Mr. Donovan, if you think I'm one of those naughty girls, you are sadly mistaken." The possibility that he would even think such a thing of her made her uncomfortable. She took her rumpled gloves from her handbag and lay them on her dresser, smoothing them out as she spoke to herself in the mirror. "Oh, well, I'll be gone from here soon after breakfast tomorrow. No need to worry on his account."

Victoria arose early to pack. She had laid aside Lily's and Agatha's belongings to be returned after breakfast, and put everything she had brought with her into the trunk. She had closed the lid and was tightening the second strap when she heard a muffled voice from the other side of her keyhole.

"Tory? It's Lily. Can I come in?"

Quickly, Victoria unbolted and unchained her door. Lily was still in her wrapper, a filmy, feminine pegnoir of pink silk hardly appropriate outside one's boudoir, let alone for an outing down the hall to the adjacent room. But Victoria was becoming accustomed to Lily's bold approach to life, and at times, even envied it.

Lily floated across the room and perched on the chair with great aplomb. "I wish we could breakfast together, but Auntie's under the weather so we won't be going to the dining room this morning. Now tell me, how was last night? And don't leave anything out," she instructed with a wag of her finger.

Victoria grinned. "You are such a snoop. Suppose I don't want to tell you about it?" she teased.

Lily drew a frown. "All right. Be that way. And after all the help I've given you because I thought we were friends."

Victoria burst into laughter. "You are a one, Lily. There's hardly anything to tell. Mr. Bartlett behaved the perfect gentleman and we waltzed for a time. Then Mr. Donovan came with a message for him, and poof! Gone. It was the old disappearing act. I never saw him again for the rest of the evening."

"Well, that's a fine thing! I've a mind to go and tell him so." Agitated, Lily rose and paced across the floor.

"You needn't bother. I'm going down at 8:30 and tell him myself." She checked her watch. 8:20. "I'm glad you stopped by. I want to thank you for loaning me these lovely things." She handed the hat, shawl and trimmings to her friend.

Lily raised her palms in refusal. "Those are yours to keep. Aunt Agatha and I insist. We don't even know why we brought them with us. We'll never use them again, not in a million years."

Victoria fingered the fine shawl. "But I couldn't possibly--"

"You could, and you will." Lily strode to the trunk, unbuckled the straps and lifted the lid. "There's plenty of room in here for everything but the hat," she stated. "Bring the other things here."

Victoria hesitated, then complied with Lily's request.

The young girl laid the goods carefully atop Victoria's clothing. "I'll bring you a box for the hat when you return from breakfast." Securing the lid once again, she headed for the door. "Lucky you, on your own. It's back to confinement for me."

As Victoria descended the grand staircase, she pondered her impending encounter with Rand Bartlett. A businesslike approach, efficient, with no reference to the previous evening seemed the best.

When she reached Mr. Donovan's office, the assistant was busy at his typewriter. Victoria knocked on the open door and stepped purposefully up to his desk. "Good morning, Mr. Donovan. I assume Mr. Bartlett is in and expecting me," she stated confidently, noting that the door to the hotel manager's office was closed.

"Miss Whitmore, good morning." He ran his fingers through the thick wave of hair at his forehead and drew a deep breath. "I'm sorry to have to tell you this, but Mr. Bartlett is in Petoskey."

Chapter 4

Stunned, Victoria searched for a logical next move. "Since Mr. Bartlett is unavailable, would you please show me to his accountant, Mr. Munson? I'm certain he can assist me."

"Again, I'm sorry, Miss Whitmore. Mr. Munson isn't in either. He departed for Petoskey yesterday afternoon."

Victoria tried to control the panic rising within her. "And when will Mr. Bartlett and Mr. Munson return?"

"That I couldn't tell you. It's possible they'll return later today, but often they're away for three days at a time."

"Three days!" Her volume rose, along with her anger.

"Yes. Mr. Bartlett manages the Arlington Hotel there, and Mr. Munson handles the accounting," he explained.

The Arlington enjoyed a widespread reputation as the finest establishment on the eastern shore of Lake Michigan. Either the Grand or the Arlington would provide a manager with full-time employment in-season, Victoria reasoned.

"Mr. Bartlett couldn't possibly manage that hotel, and this one, too," she insisted, then realized the ridiculousness of her statement. He obviously could, and did. "Pardon me. I shouldn't question your veracity, Mr. Donovan. It's just that I've been left in a very difficult situation with both Mr. Bartlett and Mr. Munson away. You're certain you have no idea when they might return?"

He shook his head. "No, I'm sorry. The matter that called them away was quite serious." Strangely, he seemed almost pleased.

"Hasn't Mr. Bartlett left instructions regarding payment to Whitmore

Furniture?"

"None at all."

"I want you to notify me the minute Mr. Bartlett or Mr. Munson returns, and not a moment later. Do you understand?"

Donovan nodded. "Yes, of course."

Victoria drew an anxious breath, realizing the burden this new delay would place on her. Shoulders erect, she leveled her gaze on Donovan. "Until then, I will occupy my room and take meals in the dining hall at the hotel's expense. It is entirely Mr. Bartlett's fault that my departure must be postponed again, and I'll not bear the cost."

"I understand, Miss Whitmore. That is only fair. I apologize for the inconvenience." Despite his words, he didn't seem the least bit sorry.

Puzzled over Donovan's behavior, and angry at the new inconvenience, Victoria walked away. Her hunger had dissipated as her anger had increased, so she decided to skip breakfast. Instead, she headed for the telegraph office, on foot this time. She had come to the island with little spending money, and must conserve as much as possible.

She couldn't help wondering whether Rand Bartlett would stop at nothing to avoid paying her. If only he had come through as promised, her money worries would have been eased considerably. Not eliminated--they would likely never reach that point--but lessened for a time. If her situation didn't improve soon, she might have to resort to borrowing from Lily's Aunt Agatha!

Her only consolation on this otherwise grim morning was the weather. Pretty mackerel clouds patterned a sky the shade of a robin's egg, and round about her she could hear the songbirds calling. The village was still waking up, the streets not yet snarled with tourists on foot or in taxis, but merchants were preparing for a busy day.

Behind Davis's grocery, fresh fruits and vegetables were being offloaded from a dray. Closer to the docks, Doud's Mercantile took delivery of dry goods.

Victoria's spirits had brightened somewhat by the time she had sent her message from the telegraph office and started walking back up the long hill.

But when she turned the key in the lock, she realized the prospect of whiling away another day waiting upon Mr. Rand Bartlett was an unwelcome one indeed.

She had barely closed her door when, as if endowed with a sixth sense, Lily appeared, hatbox in hand.

"Breakfast must have been especially good this morning, to keep you so long," she chirped, opening the box and nestling the rose-laden straw hat in a cocoon of tissue.

"I have no idea. I didn't eat breakfast," Victoria explained somewhat sourly.

"You mean it took all this time to squeeze a check out of RB? I'm beginning to wonder if he isn't a skinflint."

"No. I mean it took all this time to discover neither Mr. Rand Bartlett nor his accountant are anywhere to be found on Mackinac, and to send Papa a message about this new delay. Mr. Bartlett and Mr. Munson have gone to Petoskey."

Lily gasped, and in her best theatrical style, slumped onto the seat of the straightback chair. "*Petoskey!* What on earth are they doing there? Why couldn't they at least have left you a check? I don't understand this at all," she complained, as if she were responsible for solving Victoria's problem.

"I don't understand it either. I can only believe that whatever it was that called Rand away from the dance last night must have been more serious than I imagined. I'm to be notified the moment he returns." Victoria removed her straw hat and laid it on the dresser, then paced across the floor.

She stared out the window at an exquisite view of the straits, but her difficulties blinded her to the scene. Victoria stood in troubled silence, pondering her predicament. She could only pray Bartlett's absence would last for hours rather than days, and that until his return, she could stretch what little remained of her thin traveling budget.

A sharp knock on her door startled her at first, then sent her flying across the room to answer it, even before Lily could pop out of her chair. Could Bartlett have returned already?

Victoria flung open the door to discover Robert, the bellboy.

"Telegram for you, Miss Whitmore."

She eagerly accepted the missive, tipped him, and closed the door, leaning her back against it.

Lily hurried to join her. "I bet it's from your wandering client," she predicted.

Victoria only stared at the envelope for a few moments. "I suppose that's possible, but he's been so inconsiderate, I can't imagine his going to the trouble to send me a telegram." Nervously, she ran her fingers over it.

"Open it, for heaven's sake," Lily urged. "The anticipation is slaying me." She leaned close, positioned to read over Victoria's shoulder.

As much as Victoria had come to appreciate Lily's friendship in the last two days, she was nevertheless reluctant to open the only telegram she had ever received beneath the eyes of the biggest snoop she had ever met. "If you'll excuse me a moment, Lily, I have a sudden urge ..."

Victoria ran across the hall to her washroom, as if answering an urgent call from nature. In privacy, she unsealed the flap and read the one-sentence message.

Its meaning sent the cold knife of fear slashing into her heart. Cotton-mouthed, she tried to speak, but could only work dry throat muscles. *Of course,* she thought. *This is the only time in my life I've ever wanted to curse, and I can't!*

"Tory, are you all right?" Lily's voice penetrated the washroom door.

Victoria pulled the chain on the flush toilet to add authenticity to her sudden disappearance, and managed to compose herself. Reluctantly she stepped out and gently guided Lily across the hall into the privacy of her room once more. "I'm as well as could be expected, considering." She handed Lily the telegram, realizing she hadn't the heart to even read it aloud.

Lily stood rooted to the spot, staring at the single sentence. "'Bank will foreclose on Friday without payment,'" she read, turning a look of grave concern on Victoria. "Today is Wednesday. That gives you only two days, Tory. *Two days!*"

Victoria's mind whirled, trying to sort out a reasonable approach to her problem. "Mr. Bartlett might come back today. Then again, he might wait until Saturday. Oh, Lily, help! I'm plumb out of ideas."

Lily's head moved slowly from side to side. "Oh, stuff! I wish I could help you, but my allowance has been cut off. I'd ask Auntie to make you a loan, but she never parts with a dime of her money unless she's provided a lengthy prospectus telling why the business is rock solid, and assuring her the investment represents minimal risk. In all honesty, your father's business is more accurately described as sitting on quicksand at the moment." She paced across the floor, chewing on her knuckle, then whirled around, eyes suddenly alight with hope. "I've got it, Tory. I know who can help you."

"Tell me, quickly."

"Mr. Michael Donovan!"

"But ... how?"

"He's perfect for you! For helping you, anyway. When we were at the dance lesson, conversation led to investments. Unlike other young women, Papa always insists I be well versed in financial matters. Anyhow, Mr. Donovan told me he's looking for investments, so he's got money. Why not ask him to make you a loan just until Bartlett comes through? I get the feeling he would find the situation quite to his liking."

Victoria put palms out. "Whoa. Slow down, Lily. I could never--"

"You could, and you will. Simply ask him to meet you to discuss business over luncheon. I don't see how he can turn you down."

Donovan offered his arm. "Shall we? The luncheon buffet is now being served and it's best to arrive early while the selection is still good."

Victoria slipped her hand onto Donovan's arm, feeling a wave of apprehension over the encounter. Though he posessed the chivalrous manners of landed gentry, his behavior of the evening before, when he had walked Victoria to her room, had put her off.

Besides, his expensive manner of dress made her feel uncomfortable. He sported a wool summer suit of the latest style for men, but she was certainly no fashion plate, having donned her pinstripe suit, which was of good quality, but plain except for the gold lady's pin Lily had loaned her.

She tried to ignore the nigglings of her subconscious and remind herself that the future of her father's business could well depend upon her ability to create the proper impression for the next hour.

The buffet table stretched fifty feet along the front lawn, offering every manner of hot or cold meat and seafood. Despite the enticing aroma of the roast beef, Victoria allowed the meat carver to place only one thin slice on her plate.

Luscious fruits, crisp vegetables, and freshly baked hot breads and rolls, were side by side with deviled eggs, tomato aspic, potato salad, Boston baked beans, and cole slaw. She helped herself to a poppyseed roll, then spooned a small portion of cole slaw onto her plate.

Mouth-watering tortes, flaky-crusted fruit and cream pies, cookies with piped frosting and colored sugar sprinkles all invited sampling, but Victoria passed them by. Her appetite had so diminished with the onset of nerves that she doubted her ability to finish the meager portions already on her plate.

Donovan chose a small table at the west end of the lawn near the garden, where the sweet fragrance of roses was growing heavy with the rise of the noonday sun. He held Victoria's white wicker chair for her.

A strong urge to walk away rose within her. *You can't leave now*, she silently scolded herself. *You've come this far; now you must see things through, for Papa's sake and your own.* Dismissing the cowardly notion, she sat down, forced a pleasant smile and determined to cut right to the heart of the matter.

"Mr. Donovan, I won't mince words with you. I'm in need of financial assistance, with the delay of the hotel's payment to my father, and you've been suggested as a source."

He smiled pleasantly. "It's possible we might be able to reach an agreement. I had no idea the new delay was causing you hardship."

"I had only considered it an inconvenience until I received a telegram from my father this morning saying the bank will foreclose Friday without another payment."

Donovan listened attentively, then sat back in his chair and studied her over the steeple of his fingers.

Victoria, having ignored her food until now, busied herself cutting into her meat. How she regretted having put the man in such a spot. *I never should have listened to Lily*, she lamented privately. *There's no reason why Donovan should want to make me a loan, temporary though it would be.* She chewed on a tiny morsel of meat, the taste of which was masked by the coppery flavor resulting from overwrought nerves.

After an interminable half-minute, Donovan leaned forward, forearms resting on the table's edge. "I'd like to help you, Miss Whitmore. Your father sounds like an honorable man, a skilled man who has worked hard for his achievements. And he has brought up a fine and lovely daughter to help him in his venture. If I am to assist you, though, it will be necessary for you to sign a portion of your father's business over to me for collateral. Once the loan and interest are paid up, the partnership agreement becomes null and void."

Victoria considered the plan. Somehow, allowing partial ownership to fall into an outsider's hands didn't appeal to her, especially when the investor's reputation was as questionable as Mr. Donovan's. Still, she needed the money, and it would only be for three days, at the most. If she missed the bank payment, there would be no more Whitmore Furniture.

"I suppose I have no alternative but to accept your proposal. If you'll draw up the agreement, Mr. Donovan, I'll sign a share of Papa's business over to you temporarily."

"It's a deal, then." He offered his hand.

Reluctantly, Victoria accepted his handshake, dismayed when he brushed a kiss across the back of her hand before releasing it. The gesture only added to her apprehension about dealing with him.

"I'm looking forward to our business relationship, Miss Whitmore. I'll draw up the documents this afternoon and send word to you when they're ready." Though his intentions seemed perfectly proper, his smile looked a bit smug. "And one thing more," he casually added, "if Mr. Bartlett doesn't come through, and you find yourself desperate to regain ownership of my share of your papa's operation, you could provide certain services I would be willing to accept in lieu of cash."

A brick of dread landed in the bottom of Victoria's stomach, and the warmth of anger flooded through her. Though she had barely touched her food, she removed the linen napkin from her lap and laid it on the table, unable to tolerate his presence any longer. Exercising great self-control, she replied sweetly, "I suppose I might be qualified to render service as bookkeeper or secretary on an hourly basis, but I doubt our arrangement will ever come to that." She knew full well it wasn't what he had meant. "I'll be expecting to hear from you. Now, if you'll excuse me."

Donovan stood with her. "Are you all right, Miss Whitmore? You're looking a bit pale. Perhaps I should see you to your room?"

"No, thank you." She put out a staying hand. "Please finish your meal. I'll see you later." So anxious was she to remove herself from his presence, she nearly ran into a waiter carrying a trayful of desserts to the buffet table.

On her way upstairs, Victoria pondered the tawdry implication of Donovan's alternative. Never would she lower herself to "service" a man as he had suggested. It certainly brought new light to his true character, despite his smooth and polished manner. Thank goodness, she would only be in his debt for a matter of hours.

Though Victoria had never been the fainting kind, she still felt hot and lightheaded, and a little shaky upon arrival at her room, and opened her windows and door to admit the cooling breeze.

Lily arrived within moments of her friend's return, floating in as if on a cloud of pink mousseline. "You weren't away long. How did your luncheon go? He agreed to make the loan, didn't he?"

Victoria tried to quell the trembling in her hands by fussing with her hair in front of the mirror. "He did. We'll meet later to sign the papers. He'll send for me when they're ready." She concluded she should not share the most troublesome aspect of the encounter with her loquacious friend.

"Wonderful! I was certain he would come through. Your troubles are over, or almost over, so why are you so fidgety? Honestly, Victoria, anybody would think you were just back from meeting the queen."

Victoria shoved a hairpin back in place and forced a smile before turning to face her friend. "I guess the whole situation has me a little more flustered than I like to admit." At least that was the truth, if not the whole of it.

"Why not take yourself on a little jaunt to town to calm your nerves? I'm certain Mr. Donovan won't be sending for you for at least a couple of hours.

"In fact, while you're there, I'd be most appreciative if you would find me something new to read. I've read Aunt Agatha's volume containing Franklin's thirteen virtues so many times, I could practically recite them from memory. 'Temperance. Eat not to dullness. Drink not to elevation. Silence. Speak not but what may benefit others or yourself. Avoid trifling conversation.' She's always reminding me of *that* one," Lily explained.

Reaching into her pocket, she handed Victoria two silver dollars. "Here's enough for the the hack fare, too, and keep the change." In a half-whisper, she explained, "I'm desperate for one of those dime novels

Auntie considers so dreadful." She winked mischievously. "And bring me a magazine to hide it in."

"But this is far too much money," Victoria argued, offering to return one of the coins. "Besides, I'd be glad to loan you *The Adventures of Huckleberry Finn.*"

Lilly shook her head. "I appreciate your offer, but I'm not in the mood for Twain. Auntie has read everything he ever wrote, and even heard Mr. Clemens lecture once. 'It's a terrible death to be talked to death.' Auntie says he delivered that line just before intermission and I ought to take it to heart, so I'll quit chattering and get back to my room. Auntie's appetite has perked up in time for a late luncheon in the garden, so I'm off to take her downstairs. Oh yes, and keep the change, Tory. Ta-ta." She breezed out with a swish of pink.

Though the prospect of buying lurid reading material held no appeal for Victoria, she couldn't help feeling a bit sorry for Lily, severely restricted by the burden of nursing her aunt through bad spells.

At least the outing has its bright side, she thought, as she gathered together parasol, handbag and gloves and locked the door. The additional coin would allow her the luxury of riding in comfort rather than walking alongside the dusty roadway.

Victoria had accomplished her mission, embarrassing though it had seemed to pay the clerk for Lily's novel, and had been in her room for an hour when her young friend stopped by.

She had come to pick up her purchases and ended up staying. She lay on Victoria's bed thoroughly engrossed in her sordid tale. Though the late afternoon was more than a little warm, Victoria had closed her door so that passersby would not peer in and find Lily sprawled out on her bed behind her awful book.

While her friend lost herself in her reading, Victoria paced the floor, waiting upon word from Donovan. Had he changed his mind, she wondered?

The thought set her nerves on edge. But so did the prospect of signing an agreement with a man she could neither trust nor respect. Still, she must go through with it or take the risk of her father being forced out of business. The possibility dominated her thoughts when an insistent knock sounded on her door.

Chapter 5

Again, the knock sounded before Victoria could even make a move to open her door.

"Coming!" She answered, wondering why a bellboy carrying Donovan's summons would be so impatient.

On the bed, Lily barely stirred.

When Victoria opened the door, she stood face-to-face with Rand Bartlett.

"Thank goodness, you're in," he exclaimed, sweeping past her into the room. "I've just returned, and came up to apologize for last night."

At the sight of Bartlett, Lily nearly bolted from the bed, slipping her book between the pages of the *Harper's Bazar* Victoria had bought her. "Mr. Bartlett, I'm Lily Atwood, a friend of Tory's." She boldly offered her hand.

"Sorry, I didn't realize Miss Whitmore had company." He pumped her hand once.

"I was just leaving," Lily explained, taking a tentative step toward the door.

Bartlett seemed to dismiss her from mind when he turned again to Victoria, taking up where he'd left off. "I never intended that you end the evening with Donovan. When he came to me, I had no idea I'd have to leave the island. But I'm back--"

"So I see," Victoria cut in, too distracted by her unexpected visitor to realize Lily was still lingering by the door. "And I certainly hope you're prepared to make your final payment, Mr. Bartlett," Victoria added sternly.

"I was just getting to that."

"Please do. And the sooner, the better."

"Let's not get hasty."

"Hasty?" Victoria echoed indignantly. "Your balance is three months overdue. Had you made payment two days ago, it could hardly qualify as hasty."

"I know, I know. But once you have your check, you'll be leaving the island, and I'd like to make your last memories of Mackinac pleasant ones. So I thought it would be nice to have a little outing. What do you say to a picnic supper with me?"

"I'm not interested in a picnic supper, Mr. Bartlett. I'm interested in a check."

"And I have it right here, Miss Whitmore." He pulled a folded paper from his inside jacket pocket and opened it with a flourish, brandishing a hotel check in front of her nose.

"That's all very impressive, Mr. Bartlett, but the check is blank."

"And for a reason. If you'll just agree to come with me, you have my word that before the evening is over, I will hand you a check made out for the full balance owed, complete with my signature."

"Is this a bribe?"

"Nothing less," he admitted, his hazel eyes alight with mischief. "I have a carriage waiting for us in the porte cochère, and the chef filling a picnic basket in the kitchen."

"I'm sorry, but I can't possibly go with you. I have other plans."

Lily stepped forward. "What Tory means, Mr. Bartlett, is that we had planned to sup together, but of course she would much rather be with you." Linking her arm with Victoria's, she pulled her toward the door. "Excuse us a moment, Mr. Bartlett."

In the hallway, Lily half-whispered, "I'll tell Mr. Donovan you won't be needing his loan after all. This is your big chance with RB, Tory!"

"But I don't *want* to have supper with him," Victoria argued, "not after the way he treated me. I just want him to make out the check and be done with it."

Lily sighed impatiently, "Humor the man, Tory. Go along with him for just this little while. Believe me, it's for the best ... for your father's sake."

She realized her friend was right. This was no time to jeopardize payment. Her father's business hung in the balance, and at least with Bartlett back so soon, she wouldn't have to fall in with the likes of Donovan. Though she would prefer to have the check made out here and now, and the business over and done with, cooperation with the delinquent hotel manager seemed a much more prudent course.

She didn't resist when Lily nudged her to return to the room and face him. "I will picnic with you if you wish, Mr. Bartlett. But understand at the outset I'm accepting your invitation only for the sake of concluding our business arrangement."

Lily somehow managed to come up with Victoria's hat, parasol, and gloves, and presented them to her. "It's all set, then. Have a pleasant outing, both of you, and I'll see you tomorrow, Tory." Her reading material held discreetly under her arm, she headed out the door. "Ta-ta!"

"It's a grand evening for an outing," Bartlett said enthusiastically, taking Victoria's key from her and locking the door behind them. Tucking her hand in his arm, he escorted her down the hall.

As she descended the staircase on the hotel manager's arm, Victoria wondered how she had allowed herself to be manipulated into her present circumstances. Realizing she might as well make the best of her situation, she gradually cleared her mind of all thoughts but those of the man at her side.

There was something about the way Rand Bartlett carried himself, she decided, that made him seem much more than just two inches taller than herself. When they passed through the rotunda and large front doorway, many guests spoke to him, not failing to notice the young woman on his arm, and in the case of several of the female guests, Victoria believed she did indeed detect a look of envy.

I'll not be influenced by the opinion others hold of him, she silently promised herself. *He has certainly not proven himself either reliable or dependable where I'm concerned.*

She did appreciate the fine, gentlemanly fashion in which he handed her up into the open brake, then unfolded and held her parasol for her with such flair. There was a touch of the showy about him tonight that made her want to chuckle, but she dared not appear amused and spoil the rapport that seemed to be improving between them.

Big John pulled the carriage out of the porte cochère and around behind the hotel. "Pardon this glimpse of the service drive, but I have to pick up the picnic basket from the kitchen. I promise more pleasant scenery for the remainder of the evening," Rand explained.

As if on cue, a young fellow stepped out of the kitchen door toting a huge wicker basket and handed it up to Bartlett.

John slapped the reins against the horse's back and once again set the carriage in motion down the drive in a northward direction.

Rand removed his jacket and laid it aside, then adjusted Victoria's parasol to shade her from the angle of the sun as it began its decline in the western sky. "First, I want to take you on the grand tour around the island. We're headed now for British Landing. It's a good place to picnic. Later, we'll tour some of the other well-known spots--Arch Rock and Sugar Loaf, then take a drive past the fort. I couldn't possibly let you go home to Grand Rapids without showing you the sights."

"I didn't come to see the sights, Mr. Bartlett--"

"Miss Victoria, I'm really rather upset with you," he interrupted, a mischievous glint in his hazel eyes. "Couldn't you grant me one small concession, seeing as how this is your last night here, and at least call me Rand or--"

"Slick?" She finished for him with a grin. "That seems most appropriate. Were it not for your repeated disappearing act, I'd have been long gone from here. I suppose, just for this evening, I could manage to call you Rand."

"Ah, that's better, Victoria." He paused, as if waiting for her to object to his use of her first name. When her response was only a slight raising of the brows, he continued. "To tell you the truth, I'm glad you aren't 'long gone from here.' I've been trying to make it up to you for all the times I haven't kept my promises."

"Do you really think that's possible, Rand? After all, I've been at wit's end trying to get you to pay up! Believe me, receiving a telegram this morning saying the bank will foreclose on my father in two days without another loan payment did nothing to calm my nerves."

A worry line furrowed his brow. "I had no idea your situation was so desperate."

"No idea?" Her voice rose with indignation. "I explained to you from the very first that my father's ability to continue in business was dependent upon your paying what you owed."

"Calm yourself, Victoria. You needn't raise your voice. I'm not going anywhere, and I can hear you perfectly well. Besides, it does nothing to enhance the mood of what is supposed to be an enjoyable outing for the both of us."

Victoria sighed. "I'm sorry, you're right. It does neither of us a bit of good and the situation is about to be resolved, so ..." she took a deep breath, trying to relax, and put on a pleasant smile, " ... you said we're going to British Landing for supper. There must be a story to go along with such a place. Perhaps you could tell me about it?"

"There's quite a story, going back to July of 1812," he explained. The shady road made her parasol unnecessary, so he folded it, then placed his arm on the seat back behind her, resting his hand lightly on her shoulder.

Victoria willed herself to relax against the seat. The gentle jostling of the carriage brought her left side into contact with Rand, and she noticed not for the first time how such nearness sent a pleasant tingle through her.

In a warm, soothing tone, Rand continued his description. "The British landed an expeditionary force at the spot where I'm taking you now. Unfortunately, Lieutenant Hanks, the commander at Fort Mackinac, didn't learn of the war until the British were already knocking at his back door.

"Hanks surrendered, and that was the end of the American effort here for two years. Then, a Major Croghan sailed up to the island. He soon discovered the fort was so high on the bluff, his cannon fire wouldn't reach it. He evidently wasn't too crafty, because he sailed north to where the British had made their landing in 1812, and I'll bet you can guess what happened after that."

"The British were waiting."

"Exactly. They fought right over there, on Dousman's farm." He leaned her way to point out the former battlefield, and Victoria noted the pleasant scent of sandalwood about him.

He was even closer to her now, the length of his leg brushing against her skirt, and she felt a magnetism emanating from him. Unable to resist its pull, she relaxed against his shoulder.

They rode on in silence for another half-mile, and just when Victoria found herself wishing they could go on like this for the rest of the evening, Big John pulled the carriage to a halt beside a long stretch of driftwood-strewn beach.

Hesitantly, as if reluctant to break contact, Rand removed his arm from behind her and reached for the picnic basket, and a blanket which had been draped over the seat in front of them. He helped Victoria from the brake. "I suppose we'd better find a good spot to spread this out," he said, handing her the blanket. He perused the shoreline. "You pick the place. Women are always so much more sensible about things like this."

Victoria was relieved to know that this picnic would be much less formal than the luncheon they had shared at Holmes Observatory; nevertheless, she laughed nervously at his request. "I'm sorry to disappoint you, but I've never chosen a picnic spot in my life. In fact, the only picnics I ever went on were along the Grand River during my childhood, and we ate wherever my father decided."

"Then it's long past time you went on such an outing, and I'm even more pleased I convinced you to come tonight. Now, where do you suppose we should spread that blanket?"

Victoria studied the beach. "There's a patch of sand yonder that's fairly free of pebbles and driftwood. What do you think?"

"I'm sure it will be fine. There. You've just become experienced in the art of picnicking on the beach."

"We haven't even opened the hamper yet, and already you're making such pronouncements. A little premature, don't you think?"

"I'm certain the affair will go swimmingly."

"Pardon?" She halted midstride, her eyes flashing from the stretch of blue water, to Rand.

He chuckled. "Poor choice of words. You needn't worry that I'm thinking of throwing you in the drink. I simply meant our outing will go well this evening. I've even bribed John to stay close at hand--but not *too* close--as a sort of chaperone to ensure my good behavior."

A backward glance told Victoria that Big John was setting up a coach table next to the parked brake. Though she hadn't perceived Rand's behavior as the least bit improper, it was comforting to know John wouldn't be far away.

They ambled down the shoreline to the sandy spot. Rand tossed aside a few pieces of wood and smoothed out the area with his foot, then helped Victoria spread out the red plaid blanket. Together, they laid out a tablecloth, removed china, crystal, and silver from the hamper, and various containers of food.

The last to come out was a bottle of white wine. Meticulously, Rand removed the cork, poured a small amount into his goblet, then swirled it around to release its bouquet before trying a taste. He nodded approval.

"It's slightly sweet. Would you care for some, Victoria?"

She had never tasted wine, or any other alcoholic beverage. But then, she had never visited Mackinac Island or found herself in the company of a gentleman such as Rand Bartlett, either.

"There's lemonade, if you'd like," he offered. "I had the chef include it, not knowing your preference."

"Lemonade would be fine," she answered, pleased at his thoughtfulness. This may be a night of firsts, but wine need not be one of them.

They served themselves from several food dishes. Delicate little cucumber sandwich appetizers, crisply fried chicken drumsticks, radishes carved into little flowers, carrot curls and stuffed celery, deviled eggs, tossed salad, fresh fruit salad--a veritable feast emerged before them. Victoria found her appetite quite up to trying some of everything, probably because she had skipped breakfast, and at lunch she had felt too sick from nerves to eat.

She finished her lemonade and Rand refilled her glass. "At least I can't be accused of plying you with alcohol on our first picnic," he observed, filling his own glass with wine and leaning back on an elbow. "Victoria, I've been meaning to ask how you became involved in your father's business. It would be natural for a son to do so, but a daughter?"

He listened with rapt attention when she explained her lack of a brother. She told of her mother's death from pneumonia, saving her father's manufactory from fire, then taking over the bookkeeping and helping to procure orders for her father whenever business went into a slump.

"Well, I've been rattling on too long," she concluded. "Tell me about yourself. Where did you grow up? Did you learn the hotel business from your father?"

An inexplicable look of hurt flitted across his features before he masked it with an artificial smile. "I grew up in Detroit, but there's not a lot to tell about it. I'd *much* rather hear how you contracted work for Grand Hotel."

Victoria sensed she mustn't press him.

"We hadn't had new orders for quite some time," she said, quickly changing the direction of the conversation, "when the work for your hotel seemed to drop into our laps. Of course, we had no way of knowing the man who ordered from us had been overspending and would soon be out of a job. It was quite a shock to learn of his replacement as manager of Grand Hotel in the *Grand Rapids News* three months ago. It can't have been easy for you coming into the position."

He set his empty wine glass aside. "If it had been easy, I wouldn't have taken the job." A smile ruffled his mouth. "I love a challenge. As manager of the Wayne in Detroit, I've already put *that* hotel in order. I was ready to add another challenge--"

Victoria put her hand palm out. "Wait. Is my mind in the clouds, or did I understand you to say you are manager of the Wayne Hotel?"

"Your mind is functioning clearly. I did indeed say I'm manager of the Wayne."

"And what about the Arlington in Petoskey? You manage that, too, according to Mr. Donovan."

"That's correct."

"You manage *three* hotels?"

He nodded.

"*One* would have been enough for most men."

He simply looked at her, his eyes dancing, his mouth curved in a self-satisfied smile.

Perhaps Victoria had been underestimating the man, with three hotels, three sets of books, three staffs of personnel to manage. And to think it took all her energy to keep one small furniture manufactory in the black! It was easier for her to understand now why the payment due her had been neglected.

"It's really a shame you won't be here this weekend." Rand's words interrupted her musings. "I'm putting on a celebration like this island has never seen before, and dozens of guests will be arriving to participate."

"No one will ever accuse you of understatement," she quipped with a grin. "I suppose you've booked the Grand to capacity."

He cocked a brow. "Close. It's going to be a big financial boon for the hotel, but I'm certain there would be no problem accommodating you, if you change your mind and stay. All day Saturday there will be contests and races--rugby, foot races, horse races, dog races, swimming, boxing--and of course the greased pole contest.

"Then the entertainments begin. German dancers from Saginaw County, Indian dancers from Chippewa County, Dutch dancers from Ottawa County, Finnish dancers from Houghton County. And last but not least, the Egyptian dancing girls."

"Egyptian dancing girls?" Victoria asked skeptically.

Rand leaned close, putting his finger to his lips, and quietly admitted, "They're really from Detroit, but don't tell anyone. Promise?"

Victoria chuckled. "Promise."

He got to his feet and paced in front of her. "A very special guest is joining us on Saturday afternoon, an important literary figure, but I can't tell you who. It's a big secret. Later, the terrace will be all lit up with colored lanterns," he spread his arms wide, "and everyone will dress their finest for the ball. There will be dancing all night long!"

He kneeled beside her on the blanket and took her hand in both of his. "I wish you were going to be there, Victoria. Say you'll stay ... on the house, of course. I could really use your help. You'd make a wonderful hostess."

She pulled her hand free. "You're wrong there. I'm about as social as an ostrich with her head in the sand, in case you hadn't noticed. I'd feel out of place; I have no experience; I haven't the slightest notion what to do in such a role."

Blast it, Bartlett thought, *has she no sensitivity at all where men are concerned?* He stared deep into gray eyes that had turned a bewitching shade of blue with the reflection of sky and water.

"I guess I'll have to spell it out for you, then." His voice was smooth and mellow as an opera tenor's. "I don't want you to leave Mackinac tomorrow, Tory." He spoke her nickname almost reverently. "I don't know why, exactly. I just know I don't want you to go. Not yet, anyway." *A little lie won't hurt,* he told himself, knowing full well he was smitten with the feisty businesswoman.

Victoria wanted to believe him, wanted to think there was something special developing between them. She enjoyed being with him. He was charming, debonair, and could set her heart aflutter with his slightest touch. More than anything, she wanted to stay on the island, but she couldn't suppress her nagging doubts.

"It sounds to me like a ploy to buy more time, to put off paying me," she said bluntly. "You've committed yourself to heavy expenses in order to mount this big weekend, and now you're strapped." She stood and looked down at him, hands on her hips. "Well, I can't give you any more time," she said evenly. "If I don't make a payment against Papa's bank loan by Friday, they'll have his business. Then, I'll have good reason not to go home," she said wryly.

She walked away, down the beach. If only she could believe he really wanted her there for more than financial reasons. That conviction would be enough to spur her to think of ways to work around her money problems--and Rand's!

He came up behind her, putting an arm about her waist and turning her toward him. "I'm not stalling payment, Tory. I said I'd write you a check, and before this evening is over, I will do just that. You sized up my situation accurately when you said I'd incurred heavy expenses for this weekend. Maybe I did overspend, but I won't renege on my word. I'd never want to be the cause of your father's business failing.

"More important, I don't ever want you to think my only interest in you is one of financial convenience. You're a very special young lady. You're headstrong, independent, intelligent, obviously a caring and devoted daughter and employee where your father is concerned."

She released herself from his touch and stepped back, hoping some distance would allow her to regain her quickly fading perspective. "You are a master of flattery, Mr. Bartlett."

"Drat it, girl. What do I have to do to prove I'm not just flattering you?" As if to answer his own question, he swept her into his arms and covered her mouth with his.

Victoria resisted mildly, pressing against his chest with her fists, but he only clung tighter. As his lips moved softly over hers, the hairs of his mustache brushed pleasantly over her skin, giving rise to little bumps along the back of her neck.

So this is what it's like to be kissed by a man, Victoria thought, the flavor of wine on her tongue. She wrapped her arms about his neck and allowed him to pull her snugly against his chest, welcoming the secure feeling it brought her.

Long moments later, their lips parted. He cradled her in his arms for several minutes, with no sound but the waves gently slapping the beach. When he released her, he took her hands in his and spent a full minute silently searching her blue-gray eyes. She dared not destroy the magic moment to question his thoughts.

He withdrew and wandered several yards down the beach, stopping to prop his foot on a log that had rolled up in a storm.

When Victoria came alongside him, she saw that he had taken the blank check and a fountain pen from his pocket and was about to use his knee for a writing table.

The romantic spell broken, she couldn't resist chuckling at what seemed a preposterous order of events. She slipped the check from him, folded it and tucked it back inside his breast pocket. "You make me feel like you've bought my kiss, which wasn't for sale at any price. Besides, before you go filling in the amount, there's something I think we should discuss."

She linked her arm in his, ambling in the direction of their blanket. "It occurs to me that we could ease both sets of financial problems for the time being if you were to pay me half your remaining balance now, and half after this big weekend is over."

Rand cast her a sidelong glance, a look of amazement evident on his face. "If you don't mind my saying so, you're the most chameleonlike woman I've ever met. Do you realize you've gone from badgering me for a check, to forcing me to put it away in less than an hour's time?" he teased. Pausing, he brought her around to face him, the tip of his finger tracing her jawline until he tenderly held her chin.

"Does this mean you'll stay, Tory?" His voice was quiet, pleading.

Chapter
6

Victoria was even surprised at her own offer--but if the truth be known, she was in no hurry to leave Rand Bartlett in her past.

She smiled up at the man who now regarded her with such tenderness, studying the strong lines of his cheek, the tense little muscle along his jawline, the tenderness in his hazel eyes. Without his jacket, his shoulders seemed even broader, his vest fitting smoothly over the expanse of his chest to nip in at his narrow waist. In her eyes, he had changed considerably since their first meeting, and no longer seemed elusive.

"I'm going to tell you a secret, Rand. When I arrived on the island, I vowed I wouldn't leave until you had paid me every penny owed. I have no intention of breaking that vow, so it appears to me, I have no choice but to stay."

"Oh, Tory!" He lifted her off the ground and swung her around, knocking her hat off and sending her hair flying from its chignon in the process.

Victoria warned, "Big John is about to come over here and take an active part in chaperoning unless you put me down this instant!"

He whirled her around one last time, then set her down and glanced in the direction of the carriage. The only visible parts of John were his feet dangling over the side of the brake.

"You're a tease, Tory. He's asleep on the job, as usual. That's why I like him."

"And you are completely untrustworthy," she accused playfully.

He retrieved her hat from the ground, brushing off particles of sand. "I know that," he admitted with a grin that gradually faded to a thoughtful look. "I know something else, too. You should never wear that beautiful dark hair of yours tucked up beneath a hat."

She took the straw boater from him, her cheeks growing warm at his compliment. An awkward moment lapsed as she tried to think of a response.

His eyes carressed her, analyzing her reaction. "Will this fetching young lady accompany me on a drive to the other side of the island? I'd like very much to show you the fort."

She smiled up at him. "I can think of nothing I would enjoy more."

They strolled down the beach to the carriage, stopping to collect picnic basket and blanket along the way.

The flaming ball eased toward the horizon, painting pinks, reds, and oranges in the western sky that reflected in muted streaks off the calm waters. Only the slightest breeze stirred, making Victoria aware again of the freshwater essence of the straits, and the subtle hint of Rand's sandalwood.

They reached the eastern side of the island as dusk turned to twilight. Moonbeams danced on the white limestone wall outlining the bastions of quiet old Fort Mackinac, an impressive, if melancholy sight. The blockhouse and officers' quarters showed no sign of life, but one pale yellow light shone forth from the guardhouse at the south sally port. Victoria remembered Scotty's explanation that the fort, nearly abandoned, had had its population reduced to eleven.

Further along, the fishing docks were quiet now, and even Main Street had grown still at this late hour. Her head on Rand's shoulder, Victoria nestled closer, seeking to ease the chill of a soft, damp breeze off the straits. He arranged his jacket over her shoulder and pulled her more snugly to him, brushing a kiss against her lips when she smiled contentedly up at him.

They were beyond the point of conversation now, Victoria thought, wanting only to memorize the feel of his solid form against hers, the warm tenderness of his arm holding her tight, the gentle softness of his mustache against her skin when his mouth covered hers.

She had allowed herself a reprieve, three more days on the island. But already she knew they would end too soon. Once home in Grand Rapids, would she be able to put this dreamlike excursion from her mind?

As John brought the brake to a stop beneath the porte cochère, she pushed the question aside, not wanting to spoil the end to a perfect evening. Rand lifted her from the carriage, keeping his hand firmly at her waist as he escorted her inside the lobby, now empty of guests, and upstairs.

At her door she turned to him and wrapped her arms loosely about his neck. He pulled her firmly to him, his hands sliding down her back to the curve of her hip. Until this night, she had given little thought to being held by a man. Rand Bartlett made her feel desirable, even beautiful.

His kiss, his embraces, the evening all seemed to be ending too soon when he finally released her. Reaching inside his breast pocket, he removed the folded check, which he had made out for half his remaining balance, and took Victoria's hand in his.

"It's been extremely pleasurable doing business with you, Tory," he half-whispered, kissing her palm before placing the check there and folding her fingers about it. "I shall look forward to making my final payment."

She searched his hazel eyes, for once filled with a steady look of sincerity. "As shall I," she answered.

Rand kissed her cheek before letting her disappear inside her door.

When Victoria emerged from her room the following morning, she encountered Lily in the hallway.

"Good morning, Lily! Guess what?" Victoria triumphantly held up Bartlett's check.

Lily seemed momentarily distracted by her own thoughts before a smile broke across her round face. "Bartlett paid you! I was sure he would. I told Mr. Donovan you wouldn't be needing his loan, but he seemed to already know. I suppose RB spoke to him before he came to your room."

"Thanks, Lily. Well, I'm off. I'm on my way to wire the money to Papa."

"You're wiring it? I ... I thought you'd just take it to him and save yourself the added expense, thrifty as you are."

"I would if I were leaving Mackinac today, but I'm staying over the weekend. I'll explain everything later. Right now, I've got to get to the telegraph office."

"I'm so glad you're staying. I'll see you later, then."

Victoria stepped out of the telegraph office and again boarded the hotel rig with Big John's assistance. She had made the bank her first stop, saving a little of Rand's payment for incidentals such as taxi fare, and wired the remainder to her father. It would be ample cash to keep the bank happy until he paid the balance.

Her ride back to the hotel beneath warm sunshine and brilliant blue skies seemed to buoy her spirits. As the buggy passed the docks she saw rustic teepees pitched by Indians who were selling their beaded moccasins, handwoven baskets, and birch bark makuks of maple sugar.

Sailing craft and steam-powered yachts were tied to the piers, and along the shoreline, rowboats and canoes. A nattily dressed gentleman in a navy blue double-breasted blazer and captain's hat was stretching a canvas awning over the stern deck of one of the yachts.

Farther along Main Street, the essence of a confectioner turning out batches of chocolates for another busy day seemed to peak Victoria's appetite, reminding her she had skipped breakfast. When Big John passed a bakery, she made him stop and wait for her while she ran inside to purchase a huge, fluffy cinnamon roll. Heedless of what others might think, she spread her handkerchief across her lap and indulged in the sweet pastry while the horse clip-clopped its way toward the base of the hill.

Tourist shops jammed both sides of the street, one with a red and white striped awning and display windows tastefully decorated with the latest in men's and women's fashion apparel. Across from it stood Foley's art gallery with its little platform jutting out from the center second floor window.

Fenton's Indian Bazaar offered mats and showshoes, effigy pipes and cornhusk dolls, while a neighbor, druggist John Bailey, touted books, stationery, guidebooks and maps.

Climbing Cadotte Avenue, Victoria inhaled the fresh-water breeze, letting it out slowly in a long, deep sigh. How relaxed she felt today, able to enjoy a brief respite from the financial worries that had beset her since before her arrival on Mackinac.

She remembered her last trip over this stretch of road beneath velvet skies, nestled against Rand. This hardly seemed the same with cabs and carriages filled with tourists everywhere she looked, but she need only close her eyes to remember the evening past, the comfort of Rand's arm about her, the gentle thrill of his lips upon hers.

She savored the memory awhile before opening her eyes to the brightness of this new day. The anticipation of actually helping Rand Bartlett, hotel manager, with his work filled her with a deep satisfaction.

The hansom entered the hotel drive and neared the porte cochère. There stood Rand, with a woman who had just alighted from the carriage ahead. His kiss on her cheek and his fond embrace suggested she was no ordinary guest. When the hotel manager's hand went to the woman's waist and he escorted her up the steps to the grand entrance, Victoria felt a prickle of jealousy.

She tipped John when he helped her down, then hurried into the hotel. Skirting the edge of the rotunda where the twosome stood talking, she continued swiftly in the direction of the stairs.

"Victoria!" Rand was calling to her.

His voice had been all too clear above the undercurrent of conversation in the lobby for her to pretend she had not heard. Turning, she managed a friendly smile as she approached him.

Rand's arm still about the woman, who was at least ten years his senior, he made introductions. "Victoria, this is Minette Richelieu, a very special friend of mine. Minette, Miss Victoria Whitmore. She and her father operate Whitmore Furniture Manufactory in Grand Rapids. They're the ones who made the new chairs in our lobby."

Minette was stunning in her garnet red broad-brimmed hat festooned with five pale fawn ostrich feathers and a black satin rosette. Beneath it, auburn hair was arranged in deep soft waves about her face and gathered loosely into a bun at the nape of her neck.

"It is my *honneur* to meet you, Miss Whitmore." Her low, silky voice held a touch of a French accent.

When the older woman's elegant hand clasped Victoria's, she became acutely aware of the soft smoothness of Minette's porcelain skin in comparison to her own. Minette's eyes, a stunning shade of deep aqua blue, glowed with a friendly inner warmth, but the prominent beauty mark on her lower left cheek detracted from them. The strong scent of her frangipani perfume permeated the air.

"I'm glad to make your acquaintance, Miss--or is it Mrs. Richelieu?"

"Call me Minette, no? And may I call you Victoria? You are Rand's friend, and so you will be mine?" Her slight squeeze of Victoria's hand confirmed her sincerity, putting the younger woman more at ease.

"Of course."

Rand explained, "I didn't think to mention last evening, Victoria, that Minette would be arriving today to help us with the weekend doings. In fact, why don't the three of us lunch together out on the front lawn? I'll ask the kitchen to prepare something special for us. Then we can discuss what must be done before Friday."

"That would be lovely," Minette agreed.

"In the meantime, Minette, I'd like to take you on a little walk around the place. Victoria, why don't you meet us on the front lawn in about an hour."

"Yes ... of course," Victoria answered, trying to accept as gracefully as possible a situation she found difficult to understand.

Minette's hand loosely on Rand's arm, the couple descended the stairs to the garden, settling onto a white wrought iron bench that offered a measure of privacy and commanded a breathtaking view of the straits. In spite of Rand's expressed need to talk with her, he now found himself somewhat at a loss for words, and gazed at distant shores while trying to organize his thoughts.

Minette's hand touched his cheek, turning him toward her. In her beautiful aqua eyes, he rediscovered the look of understanding that had always been there for him from his early adolescence. Rand squeezed Minette's hand, then laid it in her lap and rose from the bench, stopping a few yards away to lean against an oak.

A panorama of almost indescribable beauty spread before him. To the west, St. Ignace stood clearly visible on the shore of Upper Michigan; to the south, the hint of Mackinaw City's harbor and warehouses lined the water's edge.

Down on Haldimand Bay, a three-sailed Mackinac boat flew white canvas in the gentle breeze while a steamer issuing puffs of black smoke made way for the straits' open water. The scent of spruce, hemlock and cedar pollen released by the sun's warm rays carried to him on the breeze that rustled the leaves overhead and braised his skin with a re-freshing coolness.

His thoughts, however, were not on his surroundings, but on the past. He had been orphaned at five, then raised by his bachelor uncle and a warm and loving housekeeper, Nonnie. At fourteen his uncle had introduced him to the French lady.

Awkward and nervous at first, Rand soon found himself at ease with Minette. Over the years, he had come to rely on her for understanding, emotional support, and advice, especially in matters of the heart.

And he had learned much from her about the ways of women. She had taught him tenderness and caring, and the words that would unlock a lady's heart when the time was right.

One summer thirteen years ago he had put into practice everything Minette had taught him.

He had come to Mackinac on vacation. Grand Hotel had not even been built yet, and he was staying at the Iroquois. While visiting the fort, he chanced to meet a beautiful young woman from Chicago.

Inexplicably drawn to one another, they spent the next three days together. He and Daisy Taylor bicycled to Sugar Loaf, Robinson's Folly, Arch Rock, and Fort Holmes. Walking Main Street, they indulged in delectable sweets from the confectioner's, and from Wendell's Custom House, he even bought her a pair of cornhusk dolls and a makuk of maple sugar made by the Chippewa Indians.

On the third day, they rented a rowboat and took a picnic lunch to Round Island, a secluded spot where they had been allowed a rare opportunity to spend time with one another in privacy. The better he got to know her, the more he appreciated her until he was intoxicated with love for her.

But the following morning when he went to collect Daisy for another day's outings, she had already checked out of her room and departed from the island.

Half-mad trying to find her, he cajoled the hotel manager into giving him her Chicago address. He departed on the very next ferry to find her, but the address turned out to be a false lead, nothing but a vacant lot on Lawrence Avenue.

Rand inquired of everyone in the area, but could find no trace of Daisy, and finally concluded that, for her own reasons, she had probably traveled under a false name.

A feeling of emptiness, deep, black, and unrelenting, set in. Why could a love that had been so beautiful become ten times more painful than the worst hurt he had ever known?

His business associates in Detroit and his pals at the Detroit Athletic Club tried valiantly to jolly him out of his depression. They lined up women for him at every opportunity, but they proved ineffective in supplanting the memories of Daisy Taylor.

Two years passed before Rand began to work himself out of his dark pit of sadness, literally, by holding down two, sometimes three, jobs at a time, moving up gradually in the hotel business from clerk to assistant manager, and finally manager of the Wayne in Detroit.

Minette had been there for him then, when he had hurt worst. She had consoled him, cried with him. "Master of the bleeding heart," she had called him. With tea and sympathy she nursed him along, for she had also loved and lost once, and she knew what it meant to be a friend in whom Rand could confide the deepest sorrows of his heart.

He knew she would never consider him weak for being sensitive, and caring, and man enough to admit his vulnerabilities. Nor had she judged him when he finally began accepting social engagements with a vengeance, seeing as many as four different women in the space of a week. His newly acquired reputation as a cad about town seemed only to make him more desirable to the socialites, a man to watch, and to be seen with.

Over the years, his memory of Daisy had diminished, the hurt of his past healed over, but a faded scar remained, enough reminder of the emotional upheaval to make him wonder why he would risk a similar situation with someone else. But the answer was already too clear, and unavoidable.

Victoria Whitmore.

She was different in many ways from Daisy--Victoria's hair was dark where Daisy's had been quite fair; Victoria worked very hard to make her way in life where Daisy had appeared to have come from a well-to-do background; Victoria approached everything with logic and forthrightness where Daisy had taken a subtle approach, giving her an air of mystery; Victoria seemed uncomfortable in social settings where Daisy had seemed practiced, even sophisticated.

He returned to Minette, seating himself beside her. "It's Victoria," he said solemnly.

Her brows raised a fraction. "I sense something different about you when she is near."

"Ever since I met her three days ago, I can't seem to think of anything or anyone else."

The older woman's mouth curved in understanding. "It is love, no? You are in love with her."

"I don't know," he said brusquely. "I can't identify the feeling, but it's so strong I can hardly put my mind to my work. I close my eyes and she's there haunting me, her eyes changing from gray to blue to gray again, her hair begging to be touched, her sometimes-doubtful look making me want to fold her in my arms, whisper reassurances in her ear, and never let her go. It's as strong ... no, stronger than what I felt for Daisy, but not at all the same. How can it be love?" He dropped a fist against the bench top in frustration.

Minette's hand covered his clenched one. "Love has many faces, many feelings, and is never twice the same," she gently counseled. "Ask yourself this, my dear friend. Feeling as you do, can it be anything but love?"

"It can't be, because I don't want it--I won't let it--be. I'm not pre-pared, Minette," he insisted. "I'm not ready to risk the loss. I won't do it!" he stated forcefully, rising to pace the stretch of grass in front of the bench. A moment later, he stood before her. "You know how long it took me to get over Daisy. I can still remember the hurt of losing her, if I think about it." He slumped onto the bench leaning forearms against his knees, head down.

A gentle hand on his shoulder returned him from his painful reminis-cences. "Tell me honestly, what did you know about Daisy? She gave you her name--I doubt it was her real one, but she told you nothing of her true self. Except for those few days with her, she seemed not to exist.

"Victoria is real. She is here, at your hotel. You said yourself she and her papa run a furniture manufactory. This manufactory has an address somewhere in Grand Rapids, does it not? When Victoria leaves the island, she will return there, no? And you will know exactly where to find her."

"It isn't that simple. When Victoria leaves Mackinac, a part of me will go with her."

"Then you must act now to ensure she will not be away for long.

Have you told her how you feel? I have the impression she will respond favorably if you declare yourself."

"I've told her only that I didn't want her to leave just yet. That was last night, and she would have gone today if I hadn't convinced her to stay and help me with the weekend celebration. But she will depart on Monday for certain. She's devoted to her father, and he needs her help."

"Things can work out, Rand, but you must tell her. You *must* let her know the true feelings in your heart."

"But I can't. If I tell her how strongly I feel about her, she will think I'm being ridiculous. 'No one can feel that way about anyone in such a short time,' she'll tell me."

"I saw something, a spark, a hint of jealousy toward me when she saw you with me. She cares more than you imagine. It is the truth, I know it."

"If only *I* could know it."

"Ask her."

"I can't just come out and say, 'Victoria Whitmore, do you care at all for me, aside from wanting me to pay your overdue bill?'"

"So that is why she has come to the island. Rand, shame!" Minette laughed lightly.

He frowned. "It's not humorous. The moment I pay her off, she's going home."

"You must pay her, Rand. You cannot put it off simply to keep her here. No, no, you must pay her, and you must speak of your feelings. I think it would benefit you both to discuss the matter openly. And consider this. Can you afford the risk of losing her?"

Victoria wondered how she would ever live through the next hour. What place had the French woman in Rand's life? Minette was all the things Victoria could never be: expensively draped in the latest style from Paris; older and possessed of a sophisticated beauty in the classic lines of her face--high cheekbones, delicate nose and well-shaped chin.

Her wideset eyes seemed to glisten with a sort of *joie de vivre*, giving their deep aqua color an unusual sparkle, and the beauty mark on her cheek made her appearance all the more distinctive and unforgettable.

Victoria took a deep breath and exhaled slowly, telling herself to relax and enjoy her surroundings. Her days on the island would slip away quickly and there was no point spending even one hour in worry.

She continued down the walk and through the gate into the children's play area. At least a dozen or more youngsters, some barely old enough to walk, had linked hands in a circle and were playing the old favorite, Ring around the Rosy. A half dozen nannies supervised the activity, and Victoria made an impulsive decision to join in the childhood fun and forget her cares until time for luncheon.

"I have a special project for you in my office. I thought it would be best to send you there after lunch, Victoria," Rand was saying.

Victoria nodded. She sat with Rand and Minette on the terrace beneath an umbrella, their table spread elegantly with pâté en croûte, whitefish poached in wine, vegetables Parisienne, crusty sourdough bread, and fresh blueberry turnovers drizzled with vanilla glaze.

A few tables away sat the woman Big John had spoken of the day Victoria arrived on the island, Bertha Palmer. She was bedecked in ruffles of peach colored silk, her gray hair arranged in a deep wave beneath a hat heavily laden with silk flowers. She looked every inch the queen of Chicago society.

At another table, Donovan was concluding a conversation with a gentleman Victoria thought she knew. After a few moments, she remembered him as the one she had seen stretching canvas over the stern of a yacht.

Victoria remembered the events of the previous day. How pleased she was that she had never had to sign the agreement with Mr. Donovan. She put unpleasant thoughts aside to enjoy her luncheon, taking a bite of the whitefish, tender and flaky and drenched in wine sauce. It reminded her of the taste of Rand's kiss the evening before. Would she ever know such a kiss again?

With barely a breeze stirring, Minette's pungently sweet fragrance was impossible to ignore. Victoria had never dabbed more than a drop of delicate hyacinth scent behind each ear, and couldn't help judging Minette excessive.

"Perhaps you and Rand will make use of my yacht, no?" Minette's question returned Victoria from her private meanderings. The glint in the woman's eye set Victoria to wondering if she had implied some hidden meaning.

Rand replied, "I'd love to, if Victoria will agree?"

"I ... of course." For some reason, Victoria seemed unable to give any but the expected answer.

"Good. Why don't the two of you plan something for tomorrow evening," Rand suggested. Laying his napkin aside, he added, "I have to get to work if we're going to be ready for field day. Victoria, if you'll report to Mr. Donovan, he'll get you started on the project in my office. Minette, I'm certain you'll want to refresh yourself in your suite. There are two new shops in the east wing you might enjoy if you find time." He rose and helped, first Minette, then Victoria, from their chairs.

Victoria watched the French woman move across the terrace toward the hotel entrance. So graceful, flowing, elegant was her carriage, with head erect, shoulders back, the ostrich feathers on her hat barely fluttering.

Victoria took one last look at the harbor, then started for Donovan's office. She had promised she would help Rand, and working in the manager's office would not be the same as working with Donovan directly.

Nevertheless, there were bound to be some awkward moments.

Chapter
7

Victoria squared her shoulders, forced a smile and knocked on Donovan's open door. The moderate rhythm of his typing came to a halt.

"Miss Whitmore, come in." His congenial manner put her at ease.

She wondered why she had been dreading the encounter. "I'm sorry about yesterday."

Rising, Donovan led her by the arm toward Bartlett's office. "I knew even before Miss Atwood gave me your message that you wouldn't be needing a loan. Slick told me the minute he returned from Petoskey that he was on his way to pay you." His lip curled slightly at one corner. "I was looking forward to being in business with you," he said ruefully.

"I hope you weren't terribly inconvenienced by the change in plans. When I spoke to you over luncheon, I had no way of knowing Mr. Bartlett would issue a check in time to prevent the foreclosure."

He dismissed her apology with a quick jerk of his head. "No harm done. Now, let me show you your task for this afternoon. Slick can use your help putting names on cards. You can write with a fine hand, can't you? Most ladies seem to cultivate the skill somewhere along the way. It will look so much better than what my typewriter can do."

He ushered her into the hotel manager's office, affording Victoria her first glimpse of Rand's working quarters. To her right, the door to the hotel safe and a four-drawer oak file cabinet took up much of the wall, while two of her father's straightbacked chairs stood against the wall to the left.

The rug beneath her feet, a Turkey carpet in deep reds and browns, covered the floor of Rand's spacious room. The woodwork had been finished in old oak, and the walls painted taupe above the wainscoting.

At the far end of the room, like a showpiece, stood a magnificent walnut desk. It had the distinctive look of a Whitmore production with its deep hand-carved relief across the wide front, and, in fact, was one of the custom made pieces for which her father had been awaiting payment.

The inlay and routing of the desktop, which would have shown her father's signature in its style, was covered by stacks of paper, correspondence, magazines, receipts, and a myriad of miscellany reflecting the personality of a man who required three jobs to keep life interesting.

Behind the desk, a high-backed chair upholstered in brown leather looked inviting. Donovan held it for her, and when she sat down, she realized how easily it tipped back. She could imagine Rand sitting in it, leg crossed on knee, leaning back to chew on a pencil and ponder how he would put on the best celebration the island had ever witnessed.

Donovan rolled her into place behind the broad walnut desk. Pointing to a stack of typed index cards, he explained, "These are the reservation cards for the guests who will be arriving this weekend. These ..." he picked up another stack of cards which had been printed with a typeset message on one side, and on the other, as she saw when the assistant flipped them over, appeared an engraving of Grand Hotel, "are special cards being issued to the wives of our guests. I need you to carefully hand-letter the name of each wife and husband in the appropriate spaces on the card, then place it in the stack behind the reservation card, keeping them in alphabetical order."

"Sounds simple enough," Victoria commented, picking up one of the typeset cards to read the message.

PERMIT

This is to certify, that I, _____, the legally wedded wife of _____, do hereby permit my husband to go where he pleases and drink what he pleases, and I furthermore permit him to keep and enjoy the company of any lady or ladies he sees fit, as I know he is a good judge, and I want him to enjoy life, as he will be a long time dead.

_____
signature

She smiled in amusement, and when she looked up, she realized Donovan was studying her reaction.

"So you approve of Slick's sense of humor," he concluded unappreciatively.

"It seems fitting." Eager to change the topic, she pulled out the shallow center desk drawer in search of a pen, and found several with a variety of nibs. "Now if you'll tell me where to find some ink, I'll get to work on this."

"It's in the right hand top drawer," he informed her. "If you need anything else, I'm just a shout away."

Victoria chose a narrow nib so her writing would fit within the space provided on the card. When she had finished one, she laid it aside to dry and went on to the next, until five were lined up across the desktop, filling the available workspace.

While she waited for them to dry, she couldn't resist the urge to straighten the miscellaneous stacks of letters and notes, journals and pamphlets that threatened to take over all but the small square of blotter directly before her. She rose and went around to the front of the wide desk.

Enough printed matter had accumulated along the perimeter to fill half a file drawer, if put away properly, which she doubted would ever happen. Rand Bartlett wouldn't light in one place long enough to do that. Nor, it seemed, would Donovan take the time for such a task. Perhaps her help in organizing the clutter would be welcomed, she concluded, jogging a collection of letters into a reasonably neat bundle and laying a World's Columbian Exposition paperweight on top.

She came next to a stack of hotel journals. The issue on top had been folded open and an engraving of Grand Hotel caught her eye. She paused to read portions of the accompanying article in *Hotel World*.

> ... the Grand is kept crowded to the utmost capacity, hundreds of arrivals taking the place of those who flit to other points ... the Hotel is taking care of 500 people every night, filled to capacity, yet this year there is not a murmur. The reason for the change in sentiment is that people realize this year that the new management will do the very best possible for every guest

beneath the gables of the Grand's hospitable roof.

"Five hundred people every night?" Victoria murmured. The figure seemed high, but maybe she had underestimated the number of guests.

Donovan came in from his office and glanced at the magazine in her hand. "Did you need something?"

"No, thank you. I was just talking to myself."

He stood behind her, looking over her shoulder at the article she was reading. "Interesting reading?" he asked wryly.

She shrugged and closed the periodical. "If you're in the hotel business, I suppose."

She picked up the next magazine in the pile. Donovan eyed it curiously, then shifted his weight nervously. "I have to go out now." He started to back out of the room. "I'll return soon to see how you're coming." In an instant, he was gone.

Victoria shrugged her shoulders and turned her attention to the magazine she was holding. It, too was opened to an article on Grand Hotel. The *National Hotel Reporter* boasted:

> Profits at Grand Hotel, Mackinac, are greater than any year before, and will approach $20,000 by season's end, so promises Mr. Rand Bartlett, the new hotel manager.

A queasiness crept into Victoria's stomach. She reread the sentence to make sure she hadn't misunderstood. "Profits at Grand Hotel, Mackinac, are greater than any year before, and will approach $20,000 by season's end ..."

Profits of $20,000!

As the meaning of it sank in, Victoria felt increasingly nauseated. Rand Bartlett had been lying to her all along about the financial status of the hotel. He had been playing her for a fool, postponing payment. He had probably even wagered a bet with his accountant on how long he could put her off!

Anger surged within like a December storm whipping through the straits, its mighty wind and fury raising twenty-foot swells to lash against vessel and shoreline and send freezing spray over the gunwales to coat the very heart of the ship, *her very heart*, with a heavy layer of ice.

She was barely aware of the sound of rapid footfalls crossing the wooden floor in Mr. Donovan's office. When she looked up from the magazine, Rand was entering the room.

She shook the magazine at him. "You've been lying to me all along, feeding me a line about the poor financial condition of your hotel. And fool that I was, I swallowed the bait, hook, line, and sinker. You actually had me convinced you were strapped by all the heavy expenses for this coming weekend. Now I know it was just a game of deception on your part."

"What ever gave you that idea?" he asked, crossing the room.

"Twenty thousand dollars profit. *That's* what gave me that idea." She tapped her index finger against the glossy page. "Twenty thousand dollars!"

"Let me see that." He reached for the journal but she pulled back, warning him off with a palm out.

"Stay away from me!"

"Will you just give me the magazine so I know what you're talking about?" He spoke in a controlled tone.

"Know what I'm talking about?" she echoed contemptuously. "Ha! Don't play the innocent with me. I know better now. And to think I believed you about your strained finances. My father, who is barely one step ahead of his creditors, could well be the next victim of your little ploy to ring up big profits here at your hotel."

She rolled the magazine into a tube, tapping it across her palm as she paced back and forth in front of him. "When I think how hard Papa's worked all these years. And, when my mother, may she rest in peace, was alive she worked right alongside him. Probably even died an early death from all the days and nights she spent working in a drafty shop. It weakened her respiratory system until she caught pneumonia."

She stopped her pacing. Hands on hips, she bent forward slightly at the waist. "And now, I'm the only one left to help Papa. I've spent the last four years doing nothing else. But I can see it makes little difference to you how difficult it's been because you haven't paid us on time." She stabbed the air with the magazine for emphasis. "You'd probably run rough-shod over your own grandmother, if you had one, just to make yourself look good.

"You're the most heartless, ruthless, selfish individual I've ever encountered, and I would be happy if I never had to lay eyes on you again, *Mr. Success*."

"Now wait just a minute, Miss Know-it-all." His voice hardened. The ruddy spots on his cheeks had spread, coloring is face scarlet. "I haven't lied to you. The hotel's finances *are* strapped."

"Then how do you explain *this*?" She unrolled the magazine and slapped it against his solar plexus, then stomped out of his office.

The journal fell to the floor before Bartlett could catch it. He bent down to pick it up, rising slowly as he read words he had never seen before, false promises of profits he knew he had never made and could never realize. His own face stared back at him from a photo identifying him as the new manager of Grand Hotel.

No wonder Tory was so upset. She had been duped, as had anyone else who had read the article, by blatant lies published in a reputable journal of the hotel industry.

How could this be? How could the editor have printed such a story? He tried to think, pacing across the floor in front of his desk. His eyes lifted, catching a glimpse of the bulletin board on the wall across from his desk, and the blank space where the photo of him, the same one as in the magazine, had once been.

He remembered the day the photo had been taken down. And he remembered who had removed it.

"Donovan, you've got some mighty tall explaining to do when I catch up with you." Magazine in hand, he strode from his office determined to confront his assistant and find some answers.

Victoria leaned against her windowsill and stared out at gardens and walkways, pedestrians and carriages, shoreline and straits waters. On another occasion she could have appreciated the everchanging view. Now, it served to remind her of the disaster her trip to Mackinac had become.

How could she ever have been such a fool as to believe Rand Bartlett? He had tricked her, smooth-talked her, convinced her he was worthy of her trust. Now, to discover his lies extended beyond the realm of his accounting problems to the pages of a very slick magazine seemed the ultimate insult.

Was the world full of such dishonesty? Would she ever learn not to be so trusting?

How depressing, she concluded, that the answers were probably yes and no, respectively.

Though she wished ardently to simply pack her trunk this instant and leave the island, she would not go back on her pledge to herself to stay until full payment of her father's bill had been obtained from Rand "Slick" Bartlett.

A knock on her door interrupted her unhappy thoughts. Perhaps Lily had come to hear the latest news. She could use a sympathetic ear right now, and no one had been more understanding than Lily.

When she opened the door, she was surprised to discover Robert, the bellboy.

"Hello, Miss Whitmore." He held up a folded paper and smiled. "I have a message for you from Mr. Bartlett."

When she reached for the note, he pulled back. "But I also have strict instructions to read it aloud to you."

"That won't be necessary, Robert. I'm perfectly capable of reading it myself, you know."

"Ah, yes, I'm certain of that. But would you? Mr. Bartlett has warned me you're not pleased with him right now, and he was afraid you'd destroy his note without knowing what it said, so I'm to read it to you."

"'Dear Tory,'" he began with an air of importance, glancing up from the page to see that she was paying attention. Victoria sighed impatiently, leaning against the door jamb.

A frown flitted across his features as he read. "'I know you have every right in the world to hate me for what you think I did, but there's a very logical explanation.'" He paused to clear his throat.

"'The article you saw in *Hotel Register* was Donovan's doing, written by him without my knowledge. The situation at Grand Hotel is as I told you during our picnic, not as reported in the magazine. Donovan thought by putting the face of success on Grand Hotel, we would gain credibility with our patrons and be the better for it. *Please,*'" Robert paused, giving added emphasis, "'accept my apology for the anguish I know this has caused you.

"'Show me your forgiveness by agreeing to see me this evening. I'll call for you at eight. RB.'" Robert folded the page and held it out.

Victoria stared at the note, then at Robert.

"Well, Miss Whitmore, can I tell him you'll be ready at eight?" he asked.

Was Bartlett's version of the situation as stated in his note really true, or had Donovan been telling the truth in his articles? Perhaps the real story lay somewhere in between.

And how could Bartlett send Robert to her with the apology? She really resented his using Robert this way, but she begrudgingly credited him with knowing her well enough to realize the standard approach wouldn't have worked. Had he come himself, she would have angrily refused to listen, and had Robert handed her the note, she would indeed have ripped the message to shreds without reading it.

Straightening, she made a conscious effort to respond in a neutral tone. "You may tell Mr. Bartlett I shall expect him at eight."

Regardless of her stilted reply, a grin blossomed on Robert's face. "I'll tell him, Miss Whitmore."

Down the hall, the door to the Atwood's suite opened. Lily observed Robert's hasty departure and hurried to join her friend. "Tory, what was that all about?"

"Lily, you just wouldn't believe it!"

"Come. Tell me all." She let herself in Victoria's room, pulled her friend in behind, and closed the door.

When Victoria accompanied Lily and Agatha to the *Salle á Manger* for the evening meal at six, she hoped they would not cross paths with Minette, whose relationship to Rand she was at a loss to understand.

On previous occasions in the main dining hall, Victoria had enjoyed observing the wealthy who dined there, but tonight she purposely avoided looking at people, concentrating instead on the floor, the ceiling, the walls.

Though she had taken notice of the elegance of the *Salle á Manger* on previous occasions, she still marveled at the richness of the oil-finished oak woodwork and beautifully inlaid wooden floor. The sheer size of the two hundred-plus-foot room left a deep and lasting impression, with its rows of two-story heavy wooden columns finished in white and gold. The ceiling they supported was paneled in deep terra-cotta red to match the walls, and the beams had been finished in an exquisite green tint.

The huge French plate glass windows looking onto the portico gave exposure to the fading afternoon light, while on the balcony above the entrance, musicians offered strains of Mozart and Brahms.

A dark-skinned waiter, reputedly hired from Chicago along with several others for the summer season because of their skill, took orders for consommé barley or bisque of clams, and departed for the kitchen.

Agatha, never one to mince words, fixed her dead-eyed stare on Victoria. "Tell me what troubles you, girl."

Shaking her head slightly, Victoria opened her mouth to voice a denial, but Agatha continued.

"I'll hear no fibbing, mind you. It's written plainly on your face something's amiss and I aim to discover just what. It involves Mr. Bartlett, I'll wager."

Victoria felt her flesh color.

Lily let out a sigh. "Oh, Auntie, can't you see Tory doesn't want to discuss it? Besides, it's none of our business."

"It's all right, Lily. I don't mind," Victoria began. "Quite by accident, I came across a very disturbing article this afternoon about Mr. Bartlett's hotel operation here. In it, he claimed Grand Hotel will show a $20,000 profit this season."

"What's so disturbing about that?" the elderly woman demanded, a smile adding more cracks to her wrinkled complexion. "I just knew he was a man of substance, someone destined for success. Sounds to me like he's just what this place needed, a real whippersnapper of a manager out to drum up business, cultivate patronage from the well-fixed, make a profit for his investors. By golly, he's done it!"

"If it's true the hotel has made such a profit," Victoria countered, "then Mr. Bartlett has been lying to me about his reasons for not paying my father's bill. He's claimed all along the hotel's budget is strained just now and that's why bills haven't been paid on time. He says the article about the profits was Mr. Donovan's doing, written without his knowledge, and that it was supposed to make the hotel appear successful to attract more patrons."

She could feel a lump of emotion forming in her throat. With an eloquent lift of her shoulders, she strained to keep her voice steady, "I just don't know what to believe anymore." Her lips rolled into a thin line, and she struggled to remain dry-eyed.

Agatha arched a brow poignantly. "Some folks say success breeds success. Perhaps the article did some good. In any case, it appears Mr. Donovan overstepped his bounds. I'd be inclined to take Mr. Bartlett at his word. Regardless of what his assistant has done, I still think Rand Bartlett is an honorable man."

At Agatha's assessment, Victoria's throat muscles began to relax. "I surely appreciate your view, Mrs. Atwood. Sometimes I just don't know what to think." Though she wasn't convinced of Rand Bartlett's complete innocence in the affair, it was somewhat comforting to know the older woman's faith in him remained undaunted.

The waiter reappeared to clear away soup dishes and deliver broiled trout with lobster sauce.

Agatha eyed her portion hungrily. "Now, let's forget about our troubles and enjoy this dinner. My appetite seems better than usual this evening. Perhaps when we're finished, you ladies would agree to walk an old woman once down the veranda?" She turned a hopeful smile on Lily.

The young girl traded her frown for a look of pure affection. "Of course, Auntie. I'm willing, but Victoria mustn't linger too long after dinner. She's expecting Mr. Bartlett to call for her at eight."

"I'd love to walk the veranda with the two of you," Victoria hastened to say. She even hoped she would be late for Rand's appointment, but Agatha, sharp as she was, would probably see to it that didn't happen.

Victoria returned to her room several minutes before eight at Agatha's insistence. As usual, Lily fussed over her. Having offered yet another alternative to her plain skirt and shirtwaist combination, she had tied a lemon-yellow silk scarf about her straw boater and was now pinning a matching satin rose at the throat of Victoria's high-collared blouse.

Lily stood back to admire the effect. Glancing at Victoria's watch, her eyes widened.

"Good gracious. It's already eight o'clock. I'd better go. Now remember what Auntie said and enjoy yourself tonight, Tory." She smiled up at Victoria, then her forehead wrinkled. "You'd better practice smiling, Tory," Lily turned her friend around to face the mirror, "or RB is likely to think your best friend just met Saint Peter."

Victoria forced the corners of her mouth upward convincingly enough to warrant a nod of approval from Lily. "Thanks for helping me get ready, Lily. And be sure to thank Agatha for the rose."

Lily headed for the door. "I'll tell Auntie, and I'll be back to find out how you fared this evening. Ta-ta."

Alone, Victoria stared at herself in the mirror, her smile having lapsed into the uncertain expression that more closely mirrored her confused feelings over Rand Bartlett. Agatha's opinion of the man had assuaged her doubts temporarily, but in solitude, she found troubling thoughts willing to pop up quickly like mushrooms given darkness and fertile soil.

Something undefinable was going on between the hotel manager and his assistant, and whatever it was, it meant problems for Rand Bartlett. Victoria reviewed the circumstances leading up to her discovery of the articles. Rand's desk had been cluttered, but not in a haphazard fashion. The stacks of papers were lined up across his desktop with a certain orderliness. Yet the magazines appeared to have been folded open across the top of these neater piles, displaying the the articles she had found so disturbing. Donovan had appeared uneasy, exiting quickly when she picked up the second journal as if he didn't want to be nearby when she read about the $20,000 profits. Could Donovan have planted the magazine articles for her to find? If so, why? Was he hoping to cause a rift between her and Rand?

Possibly, the truth of the hotel's finances lay somewhere between showing a $20,000 profit, as Donovan claimed, and running so tight the accountant had to run ninety days in arrears paying bills. Almost more than anything, she dreaded discovering that funds really were available and that for some unknown reason she had been put off in her attempts to obtain payment.

Her thoughts focused on the reflection in the mirror now, and she read the reversed image of her watch. Already, it was twenty minutes past eight. After all the fuss and bother, after being deserted by Rand, she couldn't help wondering when or even if he would appear at her door. Rand's sheer disregard for punctuality sent a surge of resentment through her.

Just when discouragement and disgust seemed to predominate, a series of loud stacatto taps sounded on her door. They could only be announcing the ever-impatient Rand Bartlett.

She stood by her dresser, unmoving. Predictably, the knocking repeated, accompanied by his vocal urgings.

"Tory? Are you there? It's me, Rand. Please open up, Tory."

He rattled the door handle impatiently, but she remained rooted in place.

Chapter
8

With deliberate movements, Victoria unlocked her door, opening it partway to reveal a gift-laden Rand Bartlett. With a nudge of his elbow, he swung the door wide on its hinges, his arms cradling a bouquet, a box, and a bottle.

"I'm sorry I'm late, Tory." The sincerity of his words couldn't be denied. He set the flowers on her dresser top, a large spray of long-stemmed red roses arranged with fern and baby's breath in a sterling silver vase.

Victoria had never received a gift of flowers, let alone long-stemmed roses. She wanted to bury her nose in them and caress their soft petals, but she would not allow Mr. Rand Bartlett to bribe his way back into her good graces.

"Your gift is lovely, but you should know it can't make up for what's happened," she said stiffly.

Ignoring her comment, he pulled one of the blossoms from the bouquet and offered it to Victoria.

"A rose for a rose, though the one I offer could not compare with your own natural beauty, Tory." The golden timbre of his voice began to melt her reserve.

Warmth suffused her cheeks until they matched the soft petals of the blossom, its sweet perfume released by a puff of moist evening air from her open window.

He set a heart-shaped, foil-wrapped candy box next to the flowers.

"Sweets for the sweet, though none could compare with your own unaffected sweetness." His mellow words flowed over her like honey.

He offered his one remaining gift, a cut crystal bottle with a red satin bow tied about its neck. "The essence of hyacinth, *your* essence, am I not correct?"

She laid the rose aside to cradle the delicate bottle in her palm, lifting the stopper slightly to release the fragrance. Small though it was, the crystal container held perfume, not a less expensive cologne or toilet water.

"I'm truly amazed you noticed my fondness for hyacinth. This is lovely, *too* lovely." She set the perfume carefully on the dresser. "You needn't have brought me anything, really. I wish you hadn't." Her last statement was only partly true, she realized, running a finger lightly over the embossed foil cover of the candy box. No one had ever indulged her like this, and she had to touch each precious gift to know she wasn't dreaming, but his generosity served only to complicate matters.

She wanted to give in to his bribery, forgive him of all that had happened and start afresh, but doubts had snagged a corner of her heart, as unwilling to release her as a barb in a fish's mouth.

Rand lifted the heart-shaped lid of the candy box and offered her a confection. Inside, an array of plump, hand-dipped creams covered with deep, dark chocolate enticed her to indulge. Each piece looked as inviting as the next, with elegant swirls on top, and she felt like a child let loose in a candy store, not knowing which to choose.

Then she remembered--once, long ago, her mother had explained how to interpret the artistic drizzles on each piece to tell which flavor cream she would find inside. She chose one with a chocolate center, extracting it ever so carefully from its paper cup.

Rand watched her bite into the confection, noting the look of pure enjoyment on her face as she savored it. He set the box aside and replaced the cover. Victoria showed immediate signs of disapproval, gesturing for him to take a piece also.

He could see from her response she had rarely, if ever received a box of good quality chocolates, and he wasn't about to deprive her of the enjoyment of even one of them.

"No, thank you. These are for you. Besides," he patted his trim waistline, "I've been so busy, I haven't been able to exercise properly. Can't risk going flabby about the middle."

Victoria popped the last half-piece of the chocolate cream into her mouth, savoring it as she turned again to the perfume. Removing the stopper, she brought it under her nose and allowed her eyes to drift shut as she inhaled. She touched the stopper once behind each ear then replaced it so carefully in the bottle that it barely made a sound.

Rand was thankful Minette had been able to recognize Tory's fragrance, but then, his French lady friend would naturally notice such details. She had suggested the flowers and candy to go with it, too, sensing a young woman as unspoiled as Tory would respond favorably to such gifts when accompanied by a sincere apology.

Tory's innocence, her lack of sophistication, her honest reactions to the world about her endeared her to him, making him determined to mend the rift caused by Donovan's misdoing.

He gestured toward the door. "Are you ready, then? I've had a runabout brought around front. It's John's night off, so I thought I'd drive the one-seater. You don't mind, do you? We could take a little ride around the island and talk. I have so many things I want to tell you."

Victoria stood before the mirror admiring the reflection of the roses, two dozen huge blossoms, wondering what Rand wanted to tell her. Was it about Minette? She was a much older, more sophisticated woman than Victoria, and obviously still held a very important place in his heart.

How she wished she had never known about Minette, or the articles in the magazines. She could have gone on in blissful ignorance enjoying her remaining days on the island and believing she meant something special to Rand.

But that was not reality, and she was a realist. She would not live a sham. Not tonight, not ever.

Rand stood by the door waiting for her. She picked up the rose he had pulled from the bouquet and took her time replacing it with the others in the vase.

Every exquisite blossom matched, belonged. Like Mrs. Palmer and the Atwoods, Rand Bartlett and Michael Donovan, even Robert, the attendant and Big John, the driver. All of them belonged here, at Grand Hotel, Mackinac Island.

She, Victoria, was the outsider, the one who didn't fit in, any more than a dandelion would fit in with glorious deep red rosebuds. Since her arrival on Mackinac Island, she had been living in a dream world, a fairy tale with a prince. And yes, even a princess, but the dream had shattered, the illusion evaporated. Only in fantasies could a fairy godmother wave her magic wand and turn a dandelion into a beautiful red rose.

Mackinac Island, as Victoria had come to learn, was no fantasyland. She was no princess, nor was Rand Bartlett the prince of her dreams. Oh, he had by no means been changed into a frog, but instead had turned out to be a real man with all-too-real personal and professional relationships.

How she wished her fairy godmother could wave a magic wand and wipe away her hurt and deceit. She didn't want Rand to think his gifts could soothe her pain, but they were beginning to do just that.

"Tory? Are you all right?"

The smooth, melodic tenor of Rand's voice, warm enough to penetrate ice, wrapped a comforting blanket over her, shielding her from the stabbing points of her icicles of concern, beckoning her to him even now.

He stayed by the door, waiting patiently. She drew on her gloves and joined him, taking one backward glance at the spray of flowers on her dresser before the door closed behind her.

"You really shouldn't have brought me anything, you know." Her words sounded distant, unreal, even to herself. Surely Rand would recognize their hollowness.

"Yes, I *should* have," Rand gently countered. He stopped in the middle of the second floor hallway to face Victoria. "I want to give you so much more. I want to make up for what's happened, to wipe away the hurt. Rand laid a finger alongside her cheek. A knife still twisted in his heart when he thought what Tory must have felt when she saw the articles.

"Tory," her name was a plea, both tender and urgent. "Can you forgive me for what happened this afternoon? I never knew about Donovan's articles. He had no right to send them off using my name. He's caused untold damage with his mistruths. The hotel owners have all been misled. But worst of all, he hurt *you*."

The look on Rand's face easily conveyed his anguish making it difficult for Victoria to doubt his words. "If what you say is true, then of course I can forgive you. You didn't have to bribe me with flowers and candy and perfume."

He was staring intently into her eyes, more gray than blue tonight, hoping their color was no indication of the atmosphere that would prevail this evening. "They were no bribe, Tory."

The huskiness in his voice, the nearness of him made her think he might kiss her right there in the hallway. She *wanted* him to kiss her, yet *didn't* want him to, all in the same moment.

Tenderly, she withdrew his hand from her cheek. Difficult as rational thought had become, somewhere down the hallway she had heard a door open and she knew she would prefer the solitude of his carriage to the second floor hallway for their intimate conversation.

"I'm glad John is off tonight," she almost whispered, "we'll be able to talk openly with one another." With a toss of her head, she turned toward the stairs, speaking in a conversational tone. "It's been such a strange day, don't you think?"

She sounded so aloof, as if they were barely acquaintances, but Rand understood. He should have known better than to show affection for Tory in the middle of the public hallway where anyone might see. He had put her, a true lady through and through, in an awkward position.

He brought his thoughts around to Tory's question. "Yes, it has been a rather unusual day, at that," he agreed, wondering exactly what she meant. As for himself, the conversation with Minette, the admission of his true feelings for Tory had already made the day memorable. Then his discovery of Donovan's ruse had nearly turned it into disaster. Thank goodness Robert had convinced Tory to accept his invitation for the evening with him.

Rand gave her a hand up into the *calèche* that awaited them beneath the porte-cochère. She pulled her skirt close as she settled on the narrow seat. No escaping contact with him in the small rig. They sat shoulder to shoulder on the tufted leather that smelled of polish, and that was so slippery she could easily slide off should the buggy come to an abrupt halt.

Victoria's slender leg brushed against Rand's muscular one as the carriage jostled along the rutted driveway, and she was again aware of the strength and warmth of him. His sandalwood scent came to her as she settled against the seat back.

Soon, they had left the hotel behind and were climbing the west bluff, passing a huge cottage that seemed more like a mansion. "Who lives there?" she couldn't help asking.

A stone foundation rose with the incline of the bluff, softened by bright pink and purple petunias. Above the rocks, a white facade, a study in scallops and points and shingles, soared three stories high, capped on each end by a turret.

"John Cudahy. Perhaps you've heard of him. He's a jolly Irish meatpacker from Chicago. Made his fortune with pork bellies and lots of hard toil. You can see his black yacht, the *Idler*, from here." Rand pointed in the direction of the harbor.

Victoria leaned forward for a better look. Sure enough, a yacht of approximately sixty feet had been tied up to one of the docks, its dark hull conspicuous in comparison to the white yachts, sailboats and rowboats.

As Rand continued along the bluff, Victoria realized Cudahy's cottage was by no means the only mansion rising to grand heights from this neighborhood. Several others had been built along this road, equally appealing with their gracefully curving verandas, and tall, pointed turrets above third-floor bedrooms.

Victoria couldn't help wondering, just for a moment, what it must be like to live in such a home, and then, only for the summer?

Such were her daydreams. Soon, she would be on the train returning to her father's apartment, and Rand Bartlett and these magnificent cottages would fade into her past.

They were off the bluff proper now, on a tree-lined northward stretch. Dusk had begun to settle over the island. The moist air, redolent with the woodsy smell of birches and maples and pines carried the lullabies of robins and sparrows as they nestled into their evening roosts.

Rand pulled off the main road and brought the buggy to a stop on a rise near the shoreline where high above, tiny pinpoints of light had begun making their ancient patterns in the darkening heavens.

He helped her from the *calèche*, but when he tried to rest his hand on her waist, she pushed it away. Free of his contact, she walked the few steps to the edge of the lookout where the music of lake meeting shoreline played a relaxing, watery rhythm. She sensed that Rand stood a few feet behind her, observing her, perhaps puzzling over what she must think of him now, tonight.

She would tell him soon enough. For now, she was determined to concentrate on the natural beauty surrounding her, this wonderland she had never, until a few days ago, known existed in Michigan. She wanted to soak in the look and feel of it, the smell and sound of it, to brand it deeply in her mind where she could call it up on a dreary summer night in a stifling city apartment.

Her eyes drifted shut and she could see it still, the vast stretch of lake water, the vanishing shreds of a sunset glistening off a gently rippling surface, the twinkling stars growing brighter in the evening's diminishing light. And the quiet anthem of forest creatures singing amen to another day played softly in her ears.

Unbidden, she began to hear, Rand's earlier apology. And with that memory came his image, a generous mouth that curved naturally upward, the strong lines of cheekbone and nose, hazel eyes sparkling with the excitement of living. She opened her eyes, ready now to turn and face the real man.

He stood watching, waiting, one hand on the horse's neck, the other hooked in his trouser pocket. *How casual, how relaxed and calm.* Her own heart tripped over a doubletime beat, lapsing into syncopation.

She inhaled deeply to the count of four while he closed the distance between them. He had no right to affect her this way. She would calm her pulse and clear her mind of irrational, emotional thoughts and tell him plainly how things stood between them.

Chapter 9

"I love you, Tory."

There, he had said it. He had practiced saying it over and over in his mind while he waited for some indication she was ready to talk.

At his words, her mind went blank. "You love me?" she echoed uncertainly. Then thoughts and questions began taking shape.

She stood perhaps two feet from him on a grassy patch a few yards from the lakeshore perimeter of the lookout. His eyes, steady on hers--had glistened and sparkled and niggled her with their mischievous look on other occasions. Now, they spoke silently and softly and tenderly the message he had delivered in words.

"I love you, Tory." He had struggled to say it the first time. The second time it was only a little easier to share the secret he must no longer keep.

"How do you know?" she asked with the innocence of a child.

How he wanted to take her in his arms, to shower her with affection, to prove in the way he knew best, by physical expressions, that he meant those words. But the changing look on her face warned him off. She hadn't yet comprehended his full meaning. And logical thinker that she was, he had best not confuse the issue with physical intimacies just yet.

"It's in here," he answered simply, a finger on his heart.

He loves me, she thought, *he loves me*. And her heart thumped crazily, mimicking the erratic popping of fireworks on the fourth of July. She no longer had to wonder what Rand Bartlett thought of her, for now she knew. He spoke the truth. She was intuitive enough to recognize it. He had made his admission without prompting or preamble. No reason existed for him to lie about those three important words.

But while her heart celebrated the news, urging her to move forward, into his arms, and confirm the ultimate emotion with an embrace, her mind raced ahead to other questions, keeping her rooted to her spot while her tongue gave them voice.

"What about Minette? Where does she fit in? You obviously care deeply about her."

"She is an old and dear friend."

"She's not *that* old."

He had to restrain himself from chuckling. Would he ever grow accustomed to Tory's frankness?

"I mean Minette has been my friend for many years. You see, I was raised mostly by my Uncle Tate Richelieu, my mother's brother.

"My father went missing back in October of '64 after the battle at Decatur, Alabama. My mother just couldn't seem to accept it. She went into a decline and doctors say she gave up wanting to live. We buried her in '66."

"But you must have been terribly young to lose both parents. Why, you couldn't have been more than five," Victoria concluded. A sensation of loneliness and fear swept over her, thinking of Rand suddenly orphaned.

He shrugged off her concern. "I was too little to really grasp it all, except to realize neither Ma nor Pa were ever coming back to take care of me.

"Thank goodness for Uncle Tate. Even though he was a kind of reckless young man living a bachelor's life, he took me to live with him. He hired an older woman, a widow with three grown children to keep house for us and watch after me. Nonnie was wonderful, everything I needed to feel secure in a world that had left me homeless.

"Then when I was fourteen, Uncle Tate met Minette, and within two months, they were married. About that time, Nonnie's daughter needed help raising her brood of five, so she moved away. From then on, Minette had a great influence over me, and I became like a stepson to her. She was never able to have her own children, and I guess that allowed us a closeness we might not have enjoyed otherwise, especially since Uncle Tate's death two years ago."

Slowly, Victoria was beginning to comprehend Minette's circumstances and her relationship with the dashing hotel manager. "So Minette is ... your widowed aunt," she concluded.

Rand nodded. "A very beautiful, desirable, wealthy widow. A Detroit businessman by the name of Monsieur La Roche has been courting her as ardently as propriety would allow, and would be here with her now, were it not for pressing business matters in France." He chuckled. "Of course, Minette would not allow his absence to spoil her plans to enjoy this weekend. A trustworthy cousin of M. La Roche by the name of Vanier accompanied her to the island. He is staying with his relatives here and will escort her to the ball."

His voice grew serious, and he looked deep into her eyes. "I hope you understand now the reasons behind my fondness for Minette."

A sense of relief, and a deepened yearning to be with him urged her forward with one tiny step. "Yes. Thank you for explaining." Tentatively, she held out her hand.

He took it in both of his and raised it to his lips, kissing it with the soft brush of his mustache. His eyes sought hers, penetrating.

She answered his beseeching look with words. "I don't suppose any of this is important compared to how we feel about one another."

"And how *do* you feel about me, Tory?"

Her hand still in his, she gave a quick squeeze and disentangled her fingers, nervously smoothing away invisible wrinkles from her skirt. Eyes down, she answered haltingly. "I ... I'm not sure quite how to answer. I feel so many different things all at the same time."

"Then tell me just one of those feelings," he urged, tenderly lifting her chin with a finger.

Again, her eyes met his, now softened. In them, she saw tenderness, hope, love, and even fear. Fear that she may not love him as he claimed to love her? "I care very much for you. I may even ... I may even love you, but ..." She hated to admit her inexperience, her uncertainty about what it meant to be in love.

Did love include doubts and insecurities? Questions of trust and dependability? One moment her heart told her she loved Rand Bartlett, the next her head took over, ruling it impossible.

"But?" He waited patiently, the lift of his brow urging her to go on.

"I'm sorry. I'm confused right now. Sometimes it seems I've known you a long time. At other times, I realize maybe I don't know you at all."

"Like when you discovered the articles in the magazines this afternoon. You have a perfect right to feel exactly as you just described." Gesturing toward the bluff, he offered his arm, inviting her to walk with him.

Together, they strolled to the edge of the embankment. Night had fallen, and the heavens offered a show of lights to far surpass any Victoria had seen in the city. Moonlight danced on the lake, casting on its rippled surface an incandescent luster.

To Victoria, despite the problems she had encountered since her arrival on Mackinac, the island had become a magic place, and the special moments she had shared with Rand Bartlett--their brief time together at the dance, the picnic outing at British Landing and drive past the fort, and even tonight--had no small part in making it so. She hated to think of leaving ... she would *not* think about it, but instead would enjoy her time with the man who professed to love her.

The concept of it still shook her to the core. She gazed upon him now while he watched the lake, moonbeams casting half his face in shadow while highlighting the contours of cheek and chin and softly bristling mustache which had become precious in her sight. Leaning up, she placed a kiss in the hollow of his cheek.

He turned to face her, and even in the darkness, she could see she had pleased him with her small sign of affection. One hand behind her neck, the other at the small of her back, he bent to kiss her. Gently, his mustache brushed her lips, like a deft artist creating a delicate orchid with a fine brush. The tiny strokes, barely making contact, teased and titillated Victoria, and though they made her hungry for more, Rand did not hurry.

He nibbled at the corner of her lips and along her jawline, then returned to place his mouth over hers, bringing with his kiss the taste of wine.

She clasped her hands behind his neck as he pulled her closer, holding her tightly against him, his hand sliding downward over her lower back.

The rhythm of his breathing intensified, spilling on her cheek in short, hot blasts. His increasing tempo drew hers into a faster pace, and she leaned into him, tightening her embrace.

The hand that had been at her neck now expertly located her hat pin and removed her hat. Instinctively, Victoria reached up to remove her hairpins, loosening dark brown tresses to cascade down her back.

With his free hand, he stroked the silky curtain of her hair, then his kisses ended as gradually as they had begun, in a trail of tiny nibbles along her cheekbone.

When he pulled away, he left her warm and flushed, her pulse rushing. Her cheek nestled against his as he continued to fondle her long hair, the sensation relaxing her.

"Tory," he breathed her name, "I don't ever want you to leave."

"I don't ever want to leave," she admitted without thinking. But almost as soon as the words were out, she recognized their absurdity.

As in the past, the chilly winds of reality came creeping into her fantasy, clearing away the soft, warm clouds of her dream world. She raised her head from his shoulder to look directly into his face.

Brushing a wave of hair from his forehead, she kissed him there, then stepped out of his embrace. Working her hair back into a twist, she secured it with hairpins and claimed the hat he still held, pinning it in place.

"Regardless of what I've said, the facts remain unchanged. Come Monday I'll be heading home."

Rand took her gently but firmly by the elbows. "You don't *have* to go on Monday if you don't want to, Tory," he said earnestly.

"I don't know what you're talking about." Her tone conveyed the frustration she felt inside.

"I want you near me, Tory. Not a couple of hundred miles away where I can't see you, can't touch you, can't show you how much I care." His intense look penetrated her with the truth of his claims.

She shook her head once. "It's absurd. You have your life here. I have my life in Grand Rapids, helping Papa."

"Your father's a grown man, able to take care of himself. It's an excuse, Tory. A lame excuse not to take chances, not to explore, not to move out of your sheltered world and experience life."

With a quick upward movement, she freed herself from his grasp and stepped back. "I didn't think you could be so cruel."

"Cruel?" he taunted, closing the distance between them by half a step.

"I'm trying to do you a favor, trying to keep you from wasting your life away. Open your eyes, Tory. Look around you. Can't you see you were meant for better things than to fade away in the upstairs apartment over a furniture shop, playing the role of your father's keeper?"

Tory turned away, biting the inside of her lip to keep from feeling the pain inflicted by the truth of Rand's words. She studied the silhouette of the horse and the *calèche* in the moonlight, trying not to listen as he continued.

"Don't get me wrong. I think your father's a talented craftsman and artist. But one of his talents is keeping you obligated to looking after him. He's not being fair to you."

She whirled around, hands on hips. Leaning forward, her face came within inches of his. "*Fair*? You, of all people, are hardly qualified to recognize fairness. Do you call neglecting to pay your bills fair? Even when I came all the way up here to collect, you put me off. Fair, ha! You're the master of unfairness, Mr. Rand 'Slick' Bartlett." Her sarcasm sliced the night air.

He threw his head back and emitted a loud whoop. "You caught me there, Tory." In the darkness, she could see the cynical curve to his mouth. "It doesn't matter what you say, I still want you with me." His expression softened, his appeal grew earnest. "You could live at the hotel and work for me. I'd give you room and board and a small salary to start. You'd have your own job, your own money, your own life, instead of living as an appendage of your father."

"My own life? Hardly." She paced back and forth across the grassy patch, keeping her eyes on Rand's moonlit figure. "I'd be living *your* life, trading my role as 'an appendage' of my father, as you so aptly put it, to become an appendage of you. No, thank you, Rand. If there's one thing I've learned on this trip, it's that I don't belong here, I don't fit in. I'm neither wealthy, nor accustomed to serving the wealthy."

She stopped her pacing to stand before him, looking directly into his eyes. "What I am is a misfit, and I look forward to Monday morning when I can say good bye to all this and return to the world I know."

With a casual lift of his shoulders, he conceded, "So be it, Tory. I only hope you don't come to regret your decision when you're old and gray and a lonely spinster." He extended a hand to her. "Now let's put aside our disagreement and try to enjoy each other's company." The smooth, mellow timbre of his voice lent credibility to his words. "I promise not to bring it up again. Soon enough, you'll be gone, and I don't want us to waste any more of our precious time together."

She studied him in the moonlight. The cynical curve of his mouth had transformed to a tender half-smile, and his rigid jawline had relaxed. She felt the tension draining from her own face in response as her clenched teeth separated and her tongue came away from the roof of her mouth.

He was right. There was no point in prolonging the disagreement. Linking her hand with his, she allowed him to help her aboard the carriage.

Secretly, she admitted his offer of a job at Grand Hotel held a certain temptation. How idyllic it would be to live on Mackinac all summer long surrounded by its beauty, to be able to take a drive like this every night.

Such were only dreams. Her deep loyalty and love for her father and his business overrode any possibility of remaining on Mackinac in Rand Bartlett's employ.

Rand pulled up near Arch Rock, a 50-foot bridge of limestone rising 146 feet above the lake. In the pale moonlight, it created a magnificent, shadowy image, a souvenir specter, and Victoria wanted to remember the look of it.

Rand reached for her hands, folding them in his. "You know, this place won't be the same for me without you." Tory could barely see his face, but his mellow voice, the way he leaned forward, spoke of his sincerity.

He brought her hands to his lips, kissing one, then the other, then drew them around his neck as he pulled her into his embrace and covered her mouth with his. Though his kiss remained chaste, a warmth pulsed through Victoria, stirring deep within her a longing to remain near Rand always. His sandalwood, strengthened by the humid night air, pleasantly surrounded her.

When the kiss ended, she laid her head on his shoulder and closed her eyes, remembering how his lips felt on hers. She wanted to store away the memory to take with her to Grand Rapids come Monday. Then, in the heat of a city night, she could think back and revive these strange and wonderful feelings she had never known until Rand.

*   *   *

The bright sunshine streaking across Victoria's face woke her to a new day. She stretched arms and legs and considered remaining in bed awhile longer, but it was only a fleeting thought. Nine o'clock. She had promised Rand last night when he left her outside her door that she would come to his office promptly at ten to help with paperwork before the myriad of guests began arriving later in the afternoon.

An hour later, she found neither Rand nor Donovan in their offices, but Rand's desk was much as she had left it, strewn with the same stacks of paperwork she had planned to put away yesterday--minus the incriminating magazines. On the center lay the cards she had been filling out.

Again, she went around to the front of his desk to see whether she could file away the documents. Moments later, footsteps sounded behind her on the Turkey carpet. She turned to face Michael Donovan.

"Mr. Bartlett is looking for you. You're to go to Munson's office right away." The ruddy patches on his freckled cheeks added to the earnestness in his voice.

"But I thought--"

"I've just spoken with him and he's asked me to send you down. Come. I'll show you." She followed him out his door. "Munson's office is the second one off the hallway to the left. It's clearly marked." With a hand at the small of her back, he nudged her in that direction.

She stepped off briskly, barely giving Donovan's words a thought, until she neared the office he had described. From behind the door labeled, "Hubert Munson, Accountant," she heard a raised voice.

Surely, Rand did not mean for her to present herself in the middle of some argument. Was Donovan misleading her?

She gave thought to returning to Rand's office to file away the papers until she caught snatches of the conversation through Munson's closed door.

" ...dancing girls ... blamed foolishness ..." It had to be Munson speaking, or rather yelling. She couldn't believe she was eavesdropping. Neither could she resist listening for Rand's response, but it was too subdued for her to catch the words.

His explanation must not have pleased the accountant, who started in again. " ... lucky to stay solvent ... shouldn't have paid on that Whitmore account ..."

Shouldn't have paid on that Whitmore account. The words echoed through Victoria's mind. Had Rand followed his accountant's advice, her father would have gone out of business! Her blood raced.

The voices from behind the door grew more distinct, and she realized Rand and Munson were about to end their conversation. Quickly, she darted down the hall and around the corner. Rand would be humiliated if he should discover she had been privy to their argument.

Chapter 10

From around the corner, Victoria could hear Munson's door slam and Rand's footfalls returning to his office. She drew a deep breath and stepped purposefully up to Munson's door.

Giving three sharp taps, Victoria opened the door and stepped inside. Behind a wide, intricately carved desk, the most elaborate mahogany piece her father had ever created, sat a ponderously overweight man, his unruly dark hair held down by the strap of his green eyeshade.

Fat cheeks bulged beneath small round eyes, giving them a squinty appearance. His triple chin drooped onto a neck the girth of Victoria's thigh, unfolding as he raised his head to send her a piercing look of inquiry.

Victoria swallowed convulsively, took a deep breath, and held her head high. "I'm Victoria Whitmore." It was more a statement than an introduction. Closing the door behind her, she crossed his thickly carpeted floor with quick strides.

He rolled his chair back, giving full berth to his mammouth gut as it emerged from behind the desk. He stood and look down on Victoria from his six-foot-three height.

"So you're the little lady who charmed Bartlett into paying out hotel funds he couldn't spare." His full, deep voice matched his size. "Do you realize the cash shortage you've caused?" he boomed, leaning forward across the desk on two hands. "Because of you, this hotel is in danger of closing."

Though his snarly look intimidated her, his accusation inflamed the angry fire burning inside her, fueling her boldness. "Certainly you exaggerate. My father's bill alone couldn't be the downfall of such a grand institution as this hotel. It is unfair of you to make such an implication."

Drawing a deep breath, she copied his stance, leaning across his desk to further confront him, their faces inches apart. "In fact, quite the reverse is true. Had Rand *not* made payment, my father would now be out of business. *My father*, whose chairs grace a lobby that would otherwise appear barren."

"Now just a minute--"

"Now *you* wait just a minute, Mr. Munson." His name was poison on her tongue. "If it weren't for Whitmore Furniture, you would have no desk from which to make your unsound judgements as to which of your creditors will or will not be paid!"

Munson pulled back. Glancing down at the desk, he seemed to regard it with pride before his eyes again met hers. "I can't be held accountable for the irresponsible expenditures of my predecessors." He sounded a bit like a whining child, and Victoria realized his blustery behavior had been all for show.

"Very convenient, blaming it on someone who's no longer here." She paced across the rug as she continued to address him. "Mr. Munson, I'll have you know I've personally expended a great deal of time and money to come here and collect the payment long overdue my father, and I will not tolerate your excuses or complaints.

"In fact, you should be grateful to me. Mr. Bartlett offered to pay me in full, but I suggested easier terms. Why, I'm even working for him without pay to help ensure the profit from this weekend!

"The very least you can do is treat me with respect, and give Mr. Bartlett the same. Monday morning, I'll expect the balance of your payment to be waiting for me when I'm ready to check out of this hotel and return to Grand Rapids. Good day, Mr. Munson."

When she arrived in Rand's office, Minette was already seated at his desk. Head bent in concentration, she was penning names on the cards Victoria had started filling out the afternoon before. A look of relief relaxed the taut lines around her bright red lips when she saw Victoria.

"I'm so glad you're here, Victoria." She sighed, setting down her pen.

"I am not much good at this, but Rand insisted I help. He worried when he did not find you here. But, now you have come and I shall gladly give the job over to you."

"I'm sorry I'm late. Something unexpected came up. I didn't mean for my work to fall to you."

"I accomplished little, I fear." Minette, outfitted in cranberry silk, rose from Rand's desk chair, every movement a study in elegance and grace. How out of place she looked in a business office, Victoria thought, in her gown of Parisian styling.

The front of her waist was accordion-pleated mousseline de soie with satin bows. The ribbons ended in pleats tucked beneath a gold-buckled belt that emphasized her trim waistline. Black guipure lace overlaid her shoulders and encrusted the deep points of silk hanging from her waist. Her skirt was narrow in front and full in back, making the soft swishing sound as only rich fabric can when she straightened and smoothed it in place.

"Rand asked me to tell you he will not be taking luncheon at the hotel today. He must see to the courses for the various races and will return much later. You will take luncheon with me, no?"

"Thank you for inviting me. I'd like that."

"Good. Perhaps you will join me in my suite? I could have luncheon served there. It would allow us more privacy, and an opportunity to discuss your outing with Rand on my yacht."

"Your suggestion sounds fine, Minette. What time?"

"One o'clock, no? Or do you need more time to finish your duty here?" She indicated the stack of cards awaiting Victoria's hand.

Victoria glanced at the work required of her, then at the clock. It was already 10:30, but, uninterrupted, she would be able to work efficiently. "I can be there at one."

"Ah, good. I shall see you then."

When Victoria entered Minette's suite, she felt as though she were being entertained like royalty. Luncheon had been set on a table near the window, offering an idyllic view.

An assortment of china and flatware covered a damask tablecloth, including individual crystal salt and pepper dishes with sterling silver feet, delicate china bouillon dishes and bone dishes, gold-plated nut and bonbon dishes, and more Victoria didn't recognize.

"Would you care for some wine?" Minette asked when Victoria had been seated. The French woman reached for a bottle from a rack beside her. "I do hope Chateau Mouton Rothschild will be agreeable?"

Victoria's first inclination was to hide her ignorance of fine wine, but she felt comfortable enough with the older woman to answer honestly.

"I should tell you I've never tasted wine in my life. My palate couldn't possibly appreciate its rare qualities. Lemonade, or just plain water are more my style, but perhaps you could describe the finer qualities of Chateau Mo ...?"

"Mouton Rothschild. It is a fine red wine, never uncorked before the meal." Minette served Victoria an imported French mineral water, then without appearing the least ungraceful, managed to ease the tight cork out of the wine bottle.

Slowly, she poured most of the rich red liquid into a transparent glass decanter which showed to advantage the claret quality of the liquid. When she had decanted the wine, she set the bottle aside, explaining, "The sediments are left in the bottle." She poured from the decanter into one of several stemmed goblets at her place.

"I'm ashamed to say," Victoria admitted, "if I were doing the pouring, I'd hardly know which glass to use."

"You needn't be ashamed. A young woman of your ... station in life ... would not have reason to know."

Victoria felt her face color. Minette reached across, touching Victoria's hand. "I do not mean to embarrass you by speaking so. I once was much like you. My family, they had little money. I came to Detroit from France years ago. Poor as, how you say, a church mouse!" She gave a little laugh, her aqua eyes twinkling.

"But no one would ever know," Victoria insisted. "Your gowns, your manners ... I feel like a fish out of water. How did you learn to fit in?"

She smiled enigmatically. "I had a mentor, a teacher who helped me. I came to this country a peasant girl from the Loire Valley with peasant manners. I took a position as servant with a very wealthy family. Soon, my employer, Mrs. Navarre, taught me everything about the rich. How they eat, how they drink, how they serve dinner for forty guests."

Victoria placed a finger on the rim of one of several still-empty glasses at her place. "If I only could learn what each of these is used for, I'd feel as though I'd come a long way."

"I will teach you, if you like."

"Would you?"

"But of course. I will teach you this, and more. Much more, if you wish."

Victoria offered a grateful smile. "Thank you, Minette. I may never need to know any of it after this weekend, but learning from you will make things go smoother."

"I am glad to tell you what I know. But first, I must ask. You will go with Rand on my yacht, no? He is so very fond of you, and eager to show you a good time while you are on the island. With John along, you will be properly chaperoned. He has a daughter nearly your age and would not allow any improprieties. Furthermore, Rand holds high regard for his driver and would not dream of putting him in a position to have to intervene on a young woman's behalf. Even so, I would offer to accompany you myself were it not for Monsieur Vanier's invitation to dine with him and his relatives."

"The outing should be properly enjoyable, as you have described it," Victoria concluded. "I'll look forward to my first experience on a yacht this evening."

"Then I shall see to arrangements for your evening meal on the *Mademoiselle*, Minette offered. "Now, let us enjoy luncheon, and I will teach you the difference between an iced tea glass and a water glass, a white wine glass and a red wine glass, a sherry glass and a liqueur glass ..."

Victoria learned not only the differences in stemmed goblets and tumblers, dishes and bowls, forks and spoons, but also the art of eating like a bird to keep her waistline slim while the men at the table gorged themselves on breads and meats, potatoes and vegetables, fruits and desserts to maintain the large bellies that indicated status and wealth. How glad she was that Rand prided himself on his trim waistline.

The more familiar Victoria became with Minette, the more at ease she felt with her. Though her first impressions had been of a sophisticated, stylish woman of the upper classes, she now realized Minette had come a long way from the peasant girl of the Loire Valley she had been twenty-five years earlier.

By three o'clock, Minette had covered thoroughly her lesson on table etiquette, and at Victoria's polite inquiry, had begun describing her experiences in Detroit. She told of her years with Rand and Tate, her adjustment to widowhood and was telling of her recent friendship with Jacque La Roche when a knock sounded on the suite door. "The bellboy has come to remove our luncheon dishes and take my instructions for your evening meal on the yacht. Please, Victoria, go to my wardrobe and look at my gowns while I confer with him. See which you think would be best for the ball."

Victoria did as Minette asked. So many gowns and petticoats hung in the wardrobe, they nearly sprang out when Victoria opened the doors.

She fawned over the fine raspberry silk skirt of one elegant dress, caught up at the back with satin bows and draped with fine netting, a scattering of seed pearls thrown in for effect. She reached for a deep aqua blue satin dress, and was admiring its design when Minette joined her.

She held a note in her hand. "Mr. Donovan has enlisted our help at the registration desk. Are you up to it, Victoria?"

"I'd be glad to do what I can," she offered, though she knew little of the procedures at a hotel registration desk aside from those she had observed while checking in the day of her arrival.

Michael Donovan came rushing over to Victoria and Minette the moment they arrived behind the registration desk.

"Thank you so much for coming down. Oh, Miss Whitmore, before I forget, here's a note from Mr. Bartlett." He handed her a folded paper.

"Thank you." She tucked the missive into her skirt pocket to read later.

Donovan ran a hand through already tousled hair. "I'm having a devil of a time with all these guests waiting for rooms. Tim can't keep up." He referred to the sandy-haired clerk who had registered Victoria on her arrival several days ago, and was now flooded with patrons eager to check in.

In spite of Victoria's misgivings about Donovan, he truly was short on staff. "I'm glad to be of help, if I can," Victoria assured him.

"Yes," Minette agreed, "show us what to do and we'll set right to work."

The assistant explained the procedure for checking guests into the vacant rooms, adding a final word of caution about one of the first-floor suites. "Mr. Bartlett is holding it in reserve for a very special patron, so we won't be able to assign it to anyone else."

Though Victoria detected a hint of curiosity on Minette's part, the French woman simply nodded. "If that is all, let us get started, then."

From Victoria's knowledge of Minette, she didn't seem the type to work behind a hotel registration desk, but the French woman possessed a diplomatic efficiency with people. Charming them with her looks and her smiles, she convinced the most argumentative patron to accept the room reserved for him, regardless of his claim it was neither what he had requested nor paid for.

If Victoria had doubted Rand Bartlett's predictions for the success of his festive weekend, she realized she was wrong. Women were amused and delighted with the "permission" cards on which she had hand-lettered their names earlier in the day.

Men, women and children of all ages talked excitedly about the races to be held on field day. Young men in particular seemed intent on entering the greased pole contest, hoping to reach the ten-dollar bill before falling into the cold straits waters.

Time passed so quickly, it was seven o'clock before Minette and Victoria had caught up with the rush at the registration desk. Victoria stopped for a moment to read Rand's note explaining he would be back by seven to take her to supper on the yacht. She looked hopefully at the open doorway to the veranda but there was no sign of him. He had probably been delayed, as usual.

Victoria took in a deep breath. The tension drained from her shoulders and neck as she slowly exhaled, but she had not even completed the relaxing exercise before her name sounded from the direction of the grand entrance.

"Tory! I want you to meet someone."

Lily was moving toward the desk on the arm of a fair-haired young man. Victoria vaguely recognized him from her first night's walk on the veranda.

The lanky fellow was flanked on the other side by Agatha, who seemed to be amused by what the gentleman was telling her. She moved a bit more sprightly than usual, a smile deepening the cracks in her aged face when she arrived at the desk.

Lily beamed, her eyes sparkling more brightly than ever. "Tory, this is Parker Haynes. Parker, Miss Victoria Whitmore, our next door neighbor up on the second floor. Tory is executive vice-president of her father's furniture company."

"Is that so?" Parker seemed impressed as he reached across the counter to shake the hand Victoria offered. He took it firmly but briefly in his. "Pleased to meet you, Miss Whitmore."

"And I, you, Mr. Haynes." This time, she didn't even blush at the fictitious title Lily assigned her but met his gaze directly. He bore the look of the well-to-do in his fashionably expensive beige wool summer suit, but his expression revealed not the haughtiness of so many of his class, but a genuine smile of warmth and pleasure.

Agatha, her pale eyes tired, but glowing, cast an admiring sidelong glance at the escort she shared with her niece. "Mr. Haynes has shown us a most delightful afternoon in the village. Why, I don't remember the last time I had such fun."

Parker smiled down at her. "I don't remember when I've enjoyed the island shops more, myself, in the company of two such charming ladies." His gaze switched to Lily, who reached up to chuck his chin.

"Watch yourself, Parker, or I'll think you're after Auntie for her money," she teased. "Tory, we're off to dine, now. Can you join us?"

"How kind of you to invite me, but I've already made plans. Perhaps another time."

Lily leaned across the counter, hand cupped to her mouth. "Mr. Bartlett?" she asked, sotto voce.

Tory nodded, though she was beginning to wonder when he would show up.

Lily's brows raised. "Enjoy your evening. I'll stop by your room later."

Another hour passed before Rand breezed in on winged feet.

"It's past time you came to take Victoria to dinner on the yacht," Minette scolded.

"I apologize for the delay. As usual, I overestimated my own efficiency and underestimated that of my stable hands," he explained.

Minette smiled. "And so it goes. Now that you are here, I will bid you and Victoria good evening and prepare for my visit with M. Vanier.

Now off with you, and have a good time," she admonished.

Rand's hand at Victoria's back, he ushered her through the grand entrance, helping her into the barouche Big John provided.

Chapter 11

The leather of the diamond-tufted seat creaked as John drove the barouche toward the harbor. Victoria leaned back, taking in the view of the ships and boats in the distance snugged against long wooden piers, and above them the brush strokes of pinks and oranges and reds fading to dusty purple as twilight doused sunset. Tonight seemed the perfect time for a cruise, a chance to relax after the rigors of the late afternoon and early evening.

Beside her, Rand held her hand but his attention was not on her. Though he was looking in the direction of the approaching shoreline, his eyes appeared unfocused, and there was a taut look to his jawline. He seemed unaware that he was alternately squeezing and relaxing his hold on her hand.

Deciding she knew him well enough now to dispense with preamble, Victoria asked, "Is something troubling you, Rand?"

His head snapped around, and she knew she had intruded on his private thoughts, but he managed a feeble smile. "I'm sorry. I didn't quite hear you."

"I asked if something was wrong. You seem worried."

"I have a slight problem. Nothing I can't handle with a some planning." He returned her hand to her lap with a reassuring squeeze and looked away again, his attention now on their approach to the wharves.

The odors of commerce were quite pronounced: of fishermen's nets and working horses; of a steamer's coal smoke and a sailor's tarred ropes.

A smokehouse emitted a pungent cloud into the night sky. The aroma of smoked fish made Victoria's mouth water, and she realized several hours had passed since her luncheon with Minette. She could almost taste smoked whitefish on her tongue, salty but not too strong.

Big John brought the rig to a halt near a slant-roofed smithy at the end of a wide pier. The crude wooden shack beside it displayed schedules for the Arnold Transit Line and numerous handbills and notices.

At the far end of the dock was heaped a monstrous pile of coal, tall enough to dwarf the man standing beside it. Victoria couldn't help wondering how many tons must be stored there for eventual transfer to yachts, excursion boats, ferries, and steamers.

"Minette's yacht is across from the black one. Do you see it?" Rand asked.

The black yacht he spoke of hugged the left side of the pier. The name *Idler* showed clearly near the bow, and Victoria remembered it was John Cudahy's boat, the one spoken of when she and Rand had driven past the meatpacker's cottage on the west bluff.

Occupying a berth opposite *Idler* was a larger white yacht. Its name, *Mademoiselle*, had been artfully applied in gold script outlined in black.

"Minette's yacht is magnificent ... like a floating palace!" Victoria answered.

Rand chuckled. "Minette would be glad to know you're impressed. She's quite proud of the old tub. When Tate was alive, they used it constantly, but since he died, she has been aboard only a few times."

He helped her alight from the carriage. To John, he said, "I'll take Miss Whitmore aboard while you park the rig."

Big John nodded. "I'll be along in a few minutes."

Rand's hand at her waist, Victoria stepped onto the dock, lifting her skirt to keep it from getting soiled. A small gangway had been extended from the *Mademoiselle*. She mounted it, leaning on Rand's arm as she stepped down onto the teakwood deck.

A canopy extended from the deck cabin amidships to the stern, and beneath it were several cushioned white wicker chairs. Rand directed her toward the cabin and held open the paneled mahogany door.

Inside was a dining saloon, furnished with a carved walnut table and matching chairs. The table had already been set with a pitcher of lemonade and ice, a bottle of wine, dishes of salads and plates of meats and relishes. Rand pulled out one of the cabriolet-legged chairs for Victoria and seated himself diagonally from her.

"I see Minette made certain our dinner would go smoothly," he said, serving Victoria lemonade. He picked up the wine bottle to read its label, then poured a portion of the pale liquid into his glass and sipped it, his eyes half-closed.

He offered a toast. "To field day and to the ball. May this be the most successful weekend ever for Grand Hotel." In spite of his optimistic words, a look of concern played about his eyes in the form of tiny wrinkles.

Victoria sipped her beverage, then set aside her glass. "Did you finish laying out the courses for the races tomorrow?" she asked, hoping to discover the cause of his worried look.

He managed a tired smile. "All set. My crew worked like the devil with me to post signs so no one will take a wrong turn." He chuckled. "I saw Robert on my way in the front door, and he threatened to go out late tonight and turn them the wrong way just to confuse matters. I told him the course was long enough without someone ending up way out on Dousman's farm instead of back at the finish line."

Learning there was no problem with the race courses, she took a more blunt approach. "I wish you would tell me what's on your mind."

Before he could respond, blasts of a tug whistle pierced the air, making conversation impossible. When they had faded away, he said, "As a matter of fact, I was a little worried about something Robert told me." Rand picked up the relish tray, arranged artfully with carrot curls and stuffed celery, carved radishes and dill sticks, and offered it to Victoria. "You must be quite hungry by now."

"I won't deny it." She took several of the carrot curls and a stalk of celery, biting into the crab meat stuffing, but after one mouthful, she resumed her line of questioning. "So what did Robert tell you that is so troubling?"

He served her a slice of cold roast beef, and one to himself before answering. "There's probably nothing to it, but he came to me a little while ago, quite concerned." He paused to take a liesurely sip of wine. "It seems Robert overheard Donovan muttering to himself when he thought he was alone, and now the bellboy's got it in his head my friend

Donovan is planning to disappear with the contents of the hotel safe sometime after the ball tomorrow night." He laughed unconvincingly. "Ridiculous, isn't it?"

The sweet carrot curl Victoria had been chewing on suddenly turned bitter, and she swallowed hastily. "Has Robert any reason to lie?"

Obvious concern replaced Rand's failed attempt at humor. "Not to my knowledge. He seemed genuinely upset when he told me. He claimed Donovan was cleaning a pistol at the time. I've never known the man to own any kind of gun, but I didn't think Robert was making it up. Donovan's been my best friend for years and I thought I knew him better than anybody else. Now I don't know what to believe."

Victoria chewed on a piece of succulent beef, thinking of a tactful way to express her unkind opinions of Rand's longtime associate. "I realize you think highly of Mr. Donovan, but I don't believe you can completely discount Robert's information. Your assistant's actions aren't above reproach, considering the magazine articles he recently had published, among other things."

"Other things? Victoria, do you know something about Donovan you should tell me?"

She mentioned the attention he had shown her the night he walked her to her room. Much to her surprise, Rand tipped his head back and laughed.

"If that isn't just like him. He's always trying to court my women friends. It's been that way between us since I can remember."

Dismayed at Rand's light treatment of the incident, Victoria continued. "His approaches go far beyond courting." She described the suggestions he had made when discussing a possible loan.

Rand's mouth tightened in a thin line. He rose from his chair and paced the length of the cabin, returning to lean his hands on the table. On his face was a look of optimism. "All I have to do is wait for Donovan to make his move. If he shows up, I'll confront him. If not, no one's the wiser for our suspicions."

"Do you think that's safe?

Rand dismissed Victoria's concern with the wave of a hand. "He'd never harm me. How could he, after all these years?" He sat at his place again and refilled each of their glasses. "To a completely successful weekend, regardless of the rumor about Donovan."

Victoria drank to Rand's toast in spite of her doubts. She thought he had highly underestimated Donovan's potential for nastiness--even violence--but it was clear Rand Bartlett was not about to take her advice on the matter.

Bay waters rippled, putting wrinkles in the shaft of yellow light cast across the black surface by the lantern on the *Mademoiselle's* port bow. It was already past nine o'clock when supper had ended and Rand and John had cast off from the dock. In the captain's seat, the coachman showed his skill at the controls of the sixty foot vessel.

The night air, heavy with moisture and tinged with coal smoke from the yacht's steam engine, teased at the errant strands from Victoria's chignon. Rand stood behind her at the port rail, his hands resting lightly on her shoulders.

As the yacht nosed out into the straits and gained speed, Victoria pulled Rand's arms tighter about her. She would never admit it to him, but she couldn't help feeling a little apprehensive on her first yacht outing. The thought of accidentally meeting with the cold black waters made her shiver, or perhaps it was just her worry for Rand, aware of the problem he would face after the ball tomorrow night.

He nudged her ear, nibbling at her lobe, sending a different sort of chill the length of her spine. It spread out to raise tiny little bumps all over her body, and soon pleasant tingling sensations filled her awareness, pushing aside worries and concerns.

Instinctively, she turned to face him, her fingers touching the auburn highlights in the brown wave at his temple, then combing through the silky strands.

He cradled her head in his hands, his lips descending to hers, then gently covering her mouth.

As if in rhythm with her heart, the vibrations of the engine quickened, each adding momentum to the other. The cool night air tugged at her sleeves and whipped at her skirt, and she pressed more tightly against Rand, absorbing a new warmth generated by a kiss that seemed to go on and on.

Victoria lost herself in the cocoon of Rand's affection, drinking in the honey of his kiss, giving herself up to the protection of his embrace. As he shielded her from the cool night air, her cares and worries blew away like motes of dust before a steady breeze. For this moment in time only the two of them existed in a heavenly world of their own creation.

Gradually, his kiss tapered off, its intense flame diminishing like the glow of a lamp being turned ever lower, ever softer until the light and heat are no longer, and the soft bristles of his mustache ceased their delicate strokes.

She laid her head against his shoulder, her back to the port rail and the dark, unfathomable night waters, and felt more secure than she could ever recall. Silly apprehensions would not spoil this rare time with Rand, for she would preserve her memories of this night to take with her when they parted.

Here with him, in his arms, she found it easy to fantasize about a time when she would never have to think of leaving. She gave in to her weariness, and in a half-sleeping state, she dreamed of a honeymoon cruise aboard a yacht such as this, of sunny days and sleepless nights, of sumptuous meals taken in the saloon and romantic evenings culminating in the privacy of a mahogany-panelled cabin.

Rand's kisses in her hair disturbed her pleasant reverie. He worked his way down over her temple until he spoke softly in her ear.

"Tory, my love, you're asleep on your feet. Come below. You can lie down in Minette's stateroom and sleep for a while if you like."

He guided her down three small steps, through a passageway to a cabin near the bow. Inside, the walls were not mahogany as in her dream, but an even more beautiful birdseye maple. Satin the shade of rose petals covered the double bed, which had been built in against the wall. Rand pulled back the cover to reveal matching satin sheets. He eased her down until she was sitting on the mattress, and he beside her, his hand caressing her cheek as he offered a chaste kiss.

When their lips parted, he stood to go and she felt strangely bereft of him, alone and lonely though he stood not two feet from her.

"I'll be on the bridge with John." His words brought her to her feet. She moved toward him, closing the gap that separated them, wrapping her arms about his neck and kissing him on the cheek.

He pulled her tightly to him, tasting her neck and sliding his hand down her back. Shivery kisses trailed across her cheek.

"Oh, Tory," he breathed, "you don't know what you do to me." He paused, drinking in the sight of her.

Her gray-blue eyes centered on the impassioned hazel ones that seemed to look through her as if viewing the window of her soul.

"I want to stay with you, Tory. Oh, how I want to stay. But the time is not right, so I must leave you before I do something I'll regret." He released her from his embrace and quickly let himself out of the cabin.

How precious he was becoming to her, how much better she would like to know him. If only their time together were not so limited! Tears welled in her eyes, and she dabbed at them with a handkerchief, swallowing past the obstinate lump in her throat.

"I will not think about the leaving," she told herself, removing her shirtwaist and skirt and laying them aside. "I will enjoy my time left with Rand, and when it is up, I will be thankful for the experience and go home to forget."

Bending down to unfasten her shoes, she worked each button free with a buttonhook from Minette's vanity. Her shoes dropped to the floor with a thud, as if to emphasize her resolve.

She slid beneath Minette's sheets and lay her head on a satin pillow, only to be filled with thoughts and feelings that wouldn't go away, longings for the man who had brought her here tonight.

The slight bump as the *Mademoiselle* arrived at her berth, and the sudden silence after the droning of engines woke Victoria from what had been a light and restless sleep. So weary she felt numb, she donned her skirt and blouse and shoes and managed to put some semblance of order to her hair with a brush found on Minette's vanity.

Rand came to the cabin for her and with John they started toward the hotel in the barouche. The ever-present stench of netted fish permeated the damp midnight air.

When the chilly temperature made Victoria shudder, Rand placed his jacket around her shoulders and pulled her snugly against him, his scent driving away the harsh odor of the waterfront.

In the privacy of the back seat, Rand's hazel eyes, visible in the yellow light of the gas lamps along the street, reflected his concern. Absent was the mischievous sparkle she had seen in them on so many occasions, replaced by a soft, caring look.

"Victoria, I've been meaning to talk to you about the ball. I'll need your help making sure everyone mingles."

"I'll do what I can," she offered hesitantly, "but I warned you earlier I haven't much experience socializing."

"What I need you to do is really very simple. A few young men at these affairs always seem to stand along the edges, never getting up the confidence to ask a young lady to go out on the dance floor. They're afraid of being turned down. You would add greatly to their enjoyment of the evening if you would be their partner."

Before she could respond, he hurried on. "The same happens with young ladies. There are always a few the fellows pay no attention to. I hate to see them standing off to the side looking forlorn, so either Donovan or I ask them to dance, then usually the other fellows do, too. It will all work out very well. Before we know it, the evening will be over and we'll both have met some interesting new people." He squeezed her hand. "But you have to promise, no matter how handsome your partners are, you'll save the last waltz for me."

Moisture gathered in Victoria's eyes, though she couldn't name any one cause. She was disappointed to think the only dance she might share with Rand would be the last one, but she was deeply touched by his genuine concern that his guests enjoy themselves.

The prospect of dancing away the evening with near stangers as partners held little appeal, but perhaps he was right. Maybe she *would* meet some interesting young fellows, though she couldn't imagine any of them being half as interesting as Rand Bartlett.

Regardless, if he needed her assistance, she would not refuse. "I'll do the best I can to help you," she offered.

He brushed a gentle kiss against her lips. "Thank you, Tory. I knew you'd understand."

Leaning back, he pulled her close. Her head came to rest in the hollow of his shoulder, and she remained content in his embrace, unwilling to stir even when the carriage halted beneath the porte cochère.

Rand helped her alight, and with his arm about her waist, escorted her through the Grand Entrance and up the curving staircase. Though he delivered her in discreet silence to her room, when he turned her key in the lock, Victoria was certain she heard a door open in the direction of the Atwood suite. Nevertheless, when she looked, she saw no sign of activity.

Dropping the key into her skirt pocket, he clasped her hands in his and pulled her close. "Get some rest, Tory," he whispered. "If you're up to it, come to the track at ten o'clock. Minette will be competing in the egg race." He kissed her forehead. "I'll see you tomorrow."

Victoria watched him go, his rapid stride carrying him down the hall. How could he be so energetic at this late hour? His pace never seemed to slacken. With a tired sigh, she entered her room.

No sooner had she slid home the bolt than three soft taps sounded, followed by three more.

"Tory, it's me." Lily's quiet announcement nevertheless penetrated the thick wood panel.

Victoria's eyelids slid shut. She didn't want to talk to anyone right now. She needed a good night's rest, if that were possible, before field day tomorrow.

"Open up, Tory, I know you're in there," Lily said a little louder this time.

Through the thick oak, Victoria half-whispered, "I'll talk to you in the morning, Lily."

"You've got to let me in, Tory," Lily pleaded. "This won't wait until morning."

Chapter 12

Reluctantly, Victoria opened her door.

Lily waltzed in, her eyes sparkling as they had when she was with Parker Haynes. "Tory, I'm so glad you're back. I've simply been *dying* to tell you all that happened on my outing today.

"Auntie and I decided to go to town, and when we got to the front door of the hotel, there was this incredibly handsome, tall dream man there arranging for a taxi." She paced the floor as she talked. "That was Parker, of course.

"Anyhow, he noticed me right away and started talking, and he said he was going down to Main Street and I said we were going to Main Street and he said if we didn't mind sharing his taxi we could all ride down together and Auntie said that would be fine--she liked him right away--and ..."

As Lily continued her explanation, Victoria undressed. By the time she had donned her nightgown, Lily had finished telling every detail of her outing with Parker, and was saying, "A little while ago when I was on my way to the kitchen to get Auntie some tea--our electric bell is out and it's impossible to get service in our room--I saw a most curious sight. Mr. Donovan was talking with a groom, I believe. I wonder what they could possibly have been discussing? I've never seen any of the grooms actually come inside the hotel before. I'm sure their quarters are above the stables, or some such.

"Well, I shall have to go now. I'll see you tomorrow. Will you be at the greased pole contest? Parker promises he'll win me a ten-dollar bill."

"I'll see you then." Victoria opened her door. "Good night, Lily."

The young girl stepped into the hall, and when the door was nearly closed, she peeked through a small slit to offer her usual, "Ta-ta."

Alone at last, Victoria crept beneath her sheets, expecting to fall asleep the moment her head hit the pillow. Instead, try as she might, she could not make sense of Donovan's situation. In the fog of Victoria's weariness, she eventually slipped into a deep sleep.

The weather couldn't have been more perfect for field day: sunshine, a balmy breeze, intense blue skies dotted with cottony puffs of clouds. Victoria had arrived a few minutes early at the track where Minette would be competing in the egg race.

Elegant ladies mounted side-saddle on prancing horses prepared for the start. Holding their reins with one hand, they were required to circle the track while balancing an egg on a silver spoon with the other.

At Rand's signal, the entrants started around the race track. Minette completed her trip around the oval, finishing several lengths ahead of her nearest competitor, winning a small silver cup.

She dismounted, drawing Victoria aside to speak with her privately.

"I am wondering, Victoria. Have you given thought to your gown for the dinner and ball this evening?"

"This evening ...?" Victoria had been so preoccupied with the field day events, she had not considered the inadequacies of her wardrobe where the ball was concerned.

Minette continued, "We are almost the same size, no? You are welcome to choose from my wardrobe any gown you wish. Please do not think me forward in offering, but I understand when you came to the island, you had planned to stay for one day, and so doing, would not be prepared for such an event. Come to my suite late this afternoon and we shall find something for you," Minette insisted.

In her aqua eyes, Victoria found a genuine warmth. "I'll see you later. Thank you."

Boxed lunches were available from the hotel for guests who preferred them, and several picnickers had already spread blankets on the beach to watch the greased pole contest by the time John drove up with Victoria and Rand.

Though the first two contestants met the cold straits waters empty-handed, Parker Haynes managed to pluck the ten dollar bill from the end of the slippery pole before intentionally diving in and swimming ashore to present his winnings to an ecstatic, admiring Lily.

When the contest was over, John drove Rand and Victoria to the start-finish line for the bicycle race at the bottom of the hill on Cadotte Avenue.

Here, two posts had been erected and a banner stretched between them marking the beginning and end of the race. Already, eager participants had positioned themselves in the starting line-up, and several supporters had gathered around to see them off.

"There's Donovan with my cycle," Rand observed as the carriage came to a halt. He helped Victoria down.

"Good luck, Rand."

He squeezed her hand. "Thanks. I'll see you later."

He claimed his bike and wheeled it into position at the starting line.

At the sound of the gun, they were off. Rand took the lead, with Donovan but a few feet behind by the time they turned the corner onto Market Street and rode out of sight.

Rand crouched low over his handlebars. He had raced Donovan many times in Detroit and they often came across the finish line within inches of one another. Like today, they usually left the rest of the pack far behind.

Though every dip in the dirt road felt like a small crater, Bartlett was making better speed than usual. He had increased the pressure in his tires last night, and it gave him a firmer, faster ride.

Down Market Street past the Astor House he rode, slowing just enough to turn left at the fort gardens.

Now he was on the uphill stretch. From the corner of his eye, he could see Donovan coming alongside, struggling to pull even.

Bartlett's breath came in short gasps as he forced his feet harder against the pedals.

Push! Push! Push! he mentally coached himself.

"I'll get you, Bartlett," Donovan threatened.

"Not a chance," Bartlett shouted in reply. Races were the always same between them, with lots of yelling back and forth. The competition had no meaning unless Donovan were there to challenge him.

The hotel manager barely made it to the top and onto the trail through the woods ahead of his rival. He swung a little wide on the curve going left into the annex. Donovan took advantage, pulling up on his left.

"Watch out, Bartlett. I'll run you off the road!" Donovan hollered.

"Try it," Bartlett challenged.

Neck and neck, they flew past the new cottage Ernst Puttkammer had been building, then past Caskey's cottage--he had built Grand Hotel in less than four months in 1887.

Bearing to the left again past the Holliday and Dunning cottages, Donovan managed to keep pace.

In a dead heat, they entered the west bluff. The road was flanked by cottages on the left, and a sharp drop-off on the right. Bartlett had ridden the route nearly every morning since May when he had moved to the island. If he had to, he could do it with his eyes closed.

They flew past Gilbert's, Amberg's, Hannah's and Hogg's. They were passing Cudahy's when Donovan warned, "Heads up! I'll run you down." Suddenly, as if to make good on his threat, Donovan swerved into Bartlett with his front tire, edging him toward the cliff.

With a skilled evasive maneuver, Bartlett managed to stay on the road and on his seat, but Donovan lost his balance, skidding in the dirt on his side, his cycle sliding off the cliff into the brush.

Bartlett abandoned his bicycle and rushed to his friend.

"What the blazes happened, pal? Are you all right?" He offered a hand, but Donovan ignored him as he scrambled to his feet.

"Get away from me, Bartlett," Donovan ground out. His brown eyes flashed amber.

"Calm down, Michael." Rand put a soothing hand on his friend's shoulder, but Donovan jerked away.

"Stay away from me!" Donovan raged.

Rand backed off. "Let's get your cycle," he suggested. He headed for the cliff. Never, had he seen Donovan so angry. It wasn't like him to take a race so seriously.

The front wheel of his assistant's cycle had caught on some under-brush a few feet down the bluff. By the time Rand reached the bike and started dragging it up to the road, Donovan was beside him, helping, as if nothing had happened.

"Thanks, Slick." He took ahold of the handlebars. "You go on. The others are starting to catch up."

Rand gave him a curious look. "This isn't like you, Donovan. I've never seen you quit before the finish--at anything."

Donovan stared at him, then straddled his bike, the familiar competitive gleam in his eyes once again. "What are you waiting for, Bartlett? I'll beat you to the finish!"

Though Donovan made a quick getaway, Bartlett managed to catch up on the downhill run, crossing the finish line a hair's breadth ahead of his assistant.

When all the contestants had completed the bicycle race, John drove Victoria to the hotel to help Minette with the dancers. Rand had gone to monitor the gentleman's yacht race and had asked her to be ready for dinner and the ball by seven.

Victoria found Minette on the front lawn of the hotel keeping the dancing acts on schedule, making certain one group followed another with a minimum of confusion and delay.

An appreciative crowd filled the lawn below the riser, applauding the young ladies clad in layers of sheer fabric which accented their breasts and encased their arms and legs.

When the last Egyptian dancer had slunk off the platform with her spangled bracelets and tinkling finger cymbals, Victoria joined Minette offstage.

"Already it is after five o'clock," the French woman noted, checking her watch. "Come. We must prepare for the dinner and the ball."

The pleasant scent of rose potpourri greeted Victoria when she entered Minette's sitting room.

"In my bedroom, I have laid out three gowns," the older woman explained. "I hope one will be to your liking." She crossed the room to the table where a bottle had been nestled in a bucket of ice.

Lifting it out, she wrapped it in a towel. "Robert remembered to chill the sherry for me. Go now, and look at the dresses. I will pour some refreshment."

In Minette's bedroom, three gowns of very different hues covered her bed. One, of intense aqua blue, seemed better suited for the attractive

French woman with its revealing decolletage and extremely narrow skirt. Beside it lay another of creamy white, and though it offered a higher neckline and more generous skirt, the color seemed wrong for Victoria when she held it up and looked in the mirror.

The third dress had taken her eye once before. Its flattering skirt consisted of raspberry silk beneath a layer of matching netting. Hundreds of tiny seed pearls added luster and elegance, and the color seemed to enhance Victoria's pale complexion.

In the mirror, she saw Minette entering the room with two glasses; one of sherry, and the other of mineral water. A look of approval was on her face. "A fine choice, Victoria. This shade of red, it does you justice, no?"

Victoria laid the dress carefully across the bed and accepted the mineral water Minette offered. "Your dress is more beautiful than any I've ever worn. You are generous to loan it to me."

Minette shrugged off the compliment. "It is nothing. Now, we shall see about our baths, then I shall help you into the gown." She set her glass aside and removed Victoria's straw boater, pulling pins out of her twist until her hair fell to her shoulders. "And I will dress your hair as well, no?"

"I would be grateful," Victoria answered.

When Victoria had finished bathing, Minette presented her with a Swanbill corset of white coutil and a lacy, embroidered petticoat of bright pink to wear beneath her gown. Over her corset, she had a belt from which to suspend her stockings of pale pink lisle--the finest Victoria had ever seen.

The bodice of her gown, separate from the skirt, was lined with pink cotton and fitted with boned darts to enhance her figure. Victoria slipped her arms through the tiny, puffed sleeves that were bound with bright pink satin ribbons. Minette tied them into bows and began fastening the ten hooks down the back hidden between delicate folds of the raspberry silk.

Victoria ran her finger over the trim of the square neckline--brilliant pink satin overlaid with creamy bobbin lace--and as she admired it in the mirror, she tried not to think how costly the outfit must have been.

With Minette's help, she slipped the skirt over her head. Lined with a strong pink cotton, it fastened with hooks to the bodice. Above the hemline ran folds of brilliant pink satin trim.

When Minette had fastened the skirt back and hooked the matching belt in place, she studied Victoria in the mirror. "It suits you, does it not?"

Victoria whirled around once as if on the dance floor. The dress flowed with her every movement, lifting to reveal stockinged feet. Minette disappeared into the closet, emerging with pink satin flat-heeled slippers. Victoria slid them on, then sat at Minette's vanity.

Working like a master with hairbrush and hairpins, ribbons and jewels, Minette swept Victoria's long dark hair away from her face, leaving the back free to make the most of her heavy, luxuriant tresses.

The finishing touch was a pearl necklace, its three strands connected with a clasp of tiny rubies set in yellow gold. Minette fastened it around Victoria's long, graceful neck.

The young woman admired her image in the mirror, then turned to Minette. "I could never thank you enough for everything you've done for me. I'll return your belongings as soon as the ball has ended. I know it will be quite late, but I hope it won't imposition you greatly. I'm certain I could never manage the hooks on the bodice by myself."

Minette touched her hand to Victoria's cheek. "Do not trouble yourself. I will be happy to help you, no matter what the hour. Now, I must ready myself. Rand and Monsieur Vanier will come to call for us soon, and I am still in my dressing gown."

Minette bathed more quickly than Victoria expected. She watched while the French woman dressed her hair, catching it up with diamond- and pearl-encrusted combs, then helped Minette into the deep aqua silk gown. Its corsage, pointed in front, was festooned with white tulle and lace, and its bottom was deeply flounced with more embroidered lace and ruched with tulle. A double garland of pearls had been fastened to the tulle with crystal pendants at the bust, curving to the right at the waist, where clasps in the form of shells held it in place. Similar garlands of pearls and crystals festooned an overskirt, crossing diagonally from the waistline to the hem.

Victoria fastened a necklace of webbed gold chain about Minette's neck. From it hung two dozen tiny diamonds and pearls.

The older woman was putting on a pair of aqua slippers when a knock sounded on her suite door. Victoria's heart gave a small leap. She couldn't help wondering how Rand would react to her, dressed in such finery.

Minette rose from her vanity stool and handed a pair of long gloves to Victoria, then pulled on her own. "We are ready, no? You look divine." She touched a finger to Victoria's chin. "Rand is waiting for you. Go now, and let him in." Minette urged her toward the door with a gentle nudge.

Somehow, she managed to pull on her gloves, unchain the door, and open it. When Rand stepped into the room, Victoria was stunned by the look of him, so dashing in his white tail coat with its roll collar showing the black silk lining of the jacket. His stiff white shirt front with studs made the most of his firm, broad chest. Its high collar brought out his strong chin and angular jaw, softened only slightly by a white bow tie.

Rand's coat was open in front, exposing the low cut waistcoat beneath and the brilliant gold chain of his pocket watch. White trousers, perfectly creased, covered his strong legs, ending at the tops of his highly polished black shoes. In one hand, he held a pair of white silk gloves, and in the other, a small velvet box.

Victoria, when he saw her, nearly took his breath away. Though he knew he could count on Minette with her astute sense of fashion and ample wardrobe to tastefully dress Victoria, he hadn't imagined how stunning the final result would be.

Victoria's new hairstyle gave her face a softer appearance, and so did the pink color he detected now flooding her cheeks.

Her red gown, neither too modest nor too revealing, contrasted with the delicate porcelain of her skin and dawn-gray of her clear eyes. The lightweight silk fabric seemed to ripple and flow with her every movement, adding grace to her willowy frame, if that were possible.

"Tory." Her name barely exceeded a whisper. Rand lay his gloves on the table and reached for her hand, bringing it to his lips.

How she wished she had not already pulled on the elbow-length gloves Minette had loaned her, for she would enjoy his affection so much more without them. Somewhere deep in her mind, a tiny voice tried to remind her proper young ladies did not think such thoughts, but she refused to listen, calling on her memories of their previous evenings together to experience again the soft tickle of his mustache and stirring warmth of his kiss.

He turned her palm up then, and inside it placed the small box of dark blue velvet.

"For you." Again, the words were whispery soft. His mouth held the slightest upward curve; his hazel eyes, the glint of anticipation, waiting for her to open his gift.

"How thoughtful. But I have nothing for you," she quietly explained, wishing desperately that on an occasion so momentous as this, she could have shared with him something of herself, if only a punched paper bookmark embroidered with the date.

"It doesn't matter. Go ahead, open it," he urged.

Victoria spent the tiniest--or was it the longest--moment wondering whether the small box contained a pin or a bracelet or ...

She lifted the lid. Nestled in the folds of navy blue velvet, a gold ring held one unblemished white pearl. The lustrous orb was neither large nor small, but of a perfectly appropriate size, Victoria thought.

"Try it on, Tory. See if it fits."

She began pulling off her right glove when he stopped her. "I had in mind you would wear it on your left fourth finger," he explained.

"Left? But ..."

"I know. That's the finger reserved for the engagement and wedding rings. I had hoped your feelings for me would warrant your wearing it on the hand closest to your heart."

Her pulse went slightly erratic. She pulled off the left glove.

Rand took the ring from its box and gently worked it over the knuckle of Victoria's fourth finger. All the while, the still small voice tried to remind her this was not a foreshadowing of things to come, but a pleasant interlude in her struggle to keep her father's business afloat.

Victoria shut away such concerns. Tonight, she would not worry about the future. Instead, she would enjoy her remaining time on the island. Soon enough, her days here would end.

She admired the pearl ring, turning it this way and that in the soft light. "How did you ever manage such a perfect fit?" she asked, impressed by the way it sat on her finger--loose enough to be comfortable but tight enough to keep the pearl upright.

"A lucky guess," Rand answered quietly, taking her hands and pulling her close. Just before his lips met hers, he whispered again, "Very lucky."

His kiss was the barest brush against her mouth, his mustache the whisper of butterfly wings telling secrets of gentleness, teasing secrets making Victoria ask for more.

She drew her arms about his neck and pressed her lips more firmly to his, tasting his sweet affection.

How Rand wished they could forgo the dinner and dance and simply go off alone together somewhere to explore the wonders of love. He envisioned the two of them alone on Minette's yacht, anchored in some safe but deserted harbor with nothing but each other and time to fill their hours.

But it was impossible. He would never compromise Victoria in that way. Besides, this was his big night, and it was just beginning. He would enjoy the celebration he had worked so hard to orchestrate for his guests, but he would be ever responsible to see that all went smoothly and no details were neglected.

Though he hated to discourage Victoria's affections, he couldn't deny the feelings of arousal rising within him. Neither could he ignore the pressing responsibilities awaiting him downstairs. He eased her hands from his neck.

"Tory, you have the most intoxicating way of kissing me," he assured her. "I feel like a drunk, wanting more all the time, but we really have to go soon, or we'll be missed at dinner."

Rand's words brought her out of her half-dream, and she felt suddenly embarrassed by the forward nature of her affections toward him. To hide her discomfort, she began pulling on her left glove. "You are right, of course. I've simply lost track of time," she admitted reluctantly.

Rand was reaching for the doorknob when a series of stacatto taps sounded. Minette came forth from the bedroom.

"It must be Monsieur Vanier," she surmised.

Rand opened the door to a distinguished-looking silver-haired gentleman with a prominent French nose. Victoria judged him to be nearing sixty.

"M. Vanier, do come in," Minette greeted. "May I introduce you to my friend, Miss Victoria Whitmore, and I believe you met Mr. Bartlett some months ago in Detroit, no?"

The dapper gentleman nodded. "So I did." Taking Victoria's hand in his, he bowed low and kissed it. "I am honored, M'amselle Whitmore."

He shook hands with Rand. "Monsieur, are you not zee crafty fellow who arranged for zee visit of Mr. Samuel Clemens to your fine hotel?"

Victoria gasped. "Samuel Clemens? Here?"

Chapter 13

Rand laughed. "M. Vanier, I guess I haven't been too crafty, since Mark Twain's stay at Grand Hotel was supposed to be a big secret. How did you know he was here?"

The older gentleman grinned. "I embarrass myself. I take wrong turn, find myself in back hallway, and there, I meet Mr. Clemens, smoking beeg cigar. No one see us. Your secret safe, Mr. Bartlett."

"How did you persuade Mr. Clemens to stay here?" Minette asked.

"When I read he would be traveling this way on his lecture tour, I wrote suggesting he reserve accommodations with us and he did. Perhaps my willingness to give him the suite at no charge had something to do with his acceptance of my invitation. I felt sorry for him. He had to declare bankruptcy after the Paige typesetter failed. Now he's on tour to earn the money to pay back all his creditors."

"How did you manage to get him here without anyone but M. Vanier finding out?" Victoria asked.

"Mr. Cudahy provided his yacht to bring the Clemenses from Mackinaw City this afternoon, and after John returned you to the hotel, he drove them up from the dock in a closed carriage and brought them in through the service entrance. They're tired from their travels and need a good rest."

"So they won't be attending the dinner and dance," Victoria concluded.

Rand checked his watch. "No, but it's time we went downstairs. Dinner is being served."

The orchestra played Vivaldi as they were being seated at their table, and soon wine glasses took on the pale shade of a dry white vintage and water glasses tinkled with ice cubes.

The dark-skinned waiters seemed even more attentive tonight than usual, if that were possible, and Victoria realized it was because she was with Rand. Swiftly, neatly, gracefully they delivered the consommé barley, then fried whitefish with tartar sauce. Relishes were served on a large silver tray: celery, olives, radishes, young onions.

The waiter served baked beans next, followed by boiled meat. It was the first time Victoria had tasted beef tongue, and she was glad when her plate, nearly untouched, was replaced with the roast meat course: short ribs of beef.

The salad course was served next, then caviar. Victoria wondered whether many people felt as she did about the fish eggs; their salty flavor and jellylike texture did little to please her. She couldn't imagine spending money on such a delicacy, though it was very popular among the wealthy.

The vegetable course seemed to be one of the few that resembled the foods she was used to eating back in her father's apartment in Grand Rapids. Nearly every day, they ate potatoes of some kind, though she had never served them *au gratin* as the chef did.

While the waiters returned to the kitchen for dessert, Rand and Victoria visited the tables of the guests. He introduced her to Bertha Honorè Palmer, the Marshall Fields, and the ebullient John Cudahy, who seemed to enjoy jabbing fun at the stone-faced Mr. Field.

Parker Haynes was seated with Lily and Agatha, and the elderly woman seemed to fully approve of her young charge's new beau.

When Rand and Victoria were seated at their table again, she hoped she would not like the dessert the waiter placed in front of her. She had already eaten more than she intended, and her corset was becoming tight.

Unfortunately, with her first taste of the Charlotte Russe, she realized she would have to resign herself to some discomfort. She could not possibly leave her portion of the layered confection uneaten.

Stars were sparkling like diamond chips in the night sky when the orchestra struck up the first dance of the ball in the terrace gardens. Multicolored lanterns swung in a gentle breeze around the perimeter of the dance floor. Paper streamers had been wrapped around lamp posts and railings and suspended in graceful swags to a lantern hanging over the center of the wooden platform.

The lilting *one*-two-three, *one*-two-three rhythm of the waltz made Victoria long to be in Rand's arms on the dance floor. Instead, per their prior agreement, she danced with a young bachelor who was too shy to find himself a partner without Rand's urging. Meanwhile, he chose as his own partner a young lady who would otherwise have sat out the dance.

Victoria marveled at how smoothly Rand had arranged the introductions and suggested the pairings for the waltz. He maneuvered so easily in such situations he seemed born to it. On the other hand, without him by her side, she was definitely feeling out of her element.

Amidst the couples crowding the dance floor, she noticed Lily, tiny and petite, was doing just fine dancing with Parker, who towered over her by a foot or more.

Seated along the edge of the dance platform with the other chaperons of young lovelies was Agatha. She conversed with the woman beside her, and Victoria thought she had never seen Agatha enjoying herself more.

The ball was coming to an end. Victoria had danced with a succession of young partners while Rand had alternated between the young women and the society matrons including Mrs. Palmer and Mrs. Field, who seemed flattered by the dashing young hotel manager's attention.

Now, the last waltz was playing, the one Victoria had waited for all evening long, and now she relished the few minutes with Rand as her partner. He held her securely in his arms, gliding smoothly through the steps as if he were a skater on a frozen pond. *One*-two-three, *one*-two-three. How she wished the piece would never end.

Around the floor, men and women seemed more graceful than they had all evening as they dipped and swooped like swans, their steps perfectly synchronized to Len Salisbury's string players. On and on and on they went, in a sort of elegant perpetual motion set to the tune of Strauss.

Too soon, the last strain had faded away, and Rand guided her from the platform. They climbed the stairs to the grand entrance and stood in the rotunda which was rustling with the sound of silks and taffetas as the ladies passed through on the way to their rooms.

Rand stopped beneath the chandelier, taking Victoria's hands in his. "I wish I could walk you upstairs, but I'm afraid I'll have to say good night here. I promised Mrs. Palmer and Mrs. Field they would be able to leave their jewels in the hotel safe immediately after the ball. Donovan and I will be quite busy for a while."

His mention of Donovan and the hotel safe brought to mind the concern he had raised on the yacht, the incident Robert had reported to him, and the horrifying thought that the assistant had plans of his own for the contents of the safe sometime later in the evening.

Alarmed at the possibility, Victoria asked in a whisper, "How do you know Robert wasn't right, that Donovan won't--"

Rand put a finger to her lips. "Don't you worry. I told you I'd be ready if he made a move. Now, I really have to go. I see Mrs. Palmer and Mrs. Field are waiting to put their jewels in safekeeping. Until tomorrow morning."

He was gone before Victoria could even bid him good night.

Bartlett leaned back in his chair and propped his feet on his desk. Around him, the room was in darkness. He had sent Donovan to the kitchen moments ago to check with the staff about Sunday's dinner menu. They would still be washing punch glasses and bowls and he had needed an excuse to get Donovan away from their offices. Rand had already bid the assistant good night in the hall and locked his office, giving the impression he would not return there until morning. Once Donovan had left, he had readmitted himself.

Maybe his precautions were a waste. Robert might have made up his tale, but he was just convincing enough to warrant the extra trouble to sidetrack Donovan for a few minutes, then sit in the dark hoping to prove the bellboy wrong.

The quiet solitude provided Bartlett his first opportunity to reflect on the incident with Donovan during the bicycle race earlier that day.

Could his friend really have intended to push him off the bluff?

The thought was troubling, particularly so when coupled with Robert's claim.

For years, Bartlett and Donovan had been such great friends, competing at the Detroit Athletic Club in boxing and swimming and cycling, trading wins.

They had even competed for the position of manager at Grand Hotel, agreeing beforehand if one was hired, he would appoint the other his assistant. Bartlett had really expected Donovan to get the top job.

They had other things in common, lady friends included. Donovan seemed to have no problem attracting the women. Many of them were social butterflies Bartlett had escorted to a party or out to dinner before losing interest. In those days, he had been recovering from losing Daisy Taylor, and he wasn't proud that he had broken a number of hearts while trying to heal his own.

Bartlett had always admired Donovan, though. He bore the polish of a Yale education--Rand had been lucky to attend Detroit College--and Donovan's clothes were always tailored to a perfect fit. Bartlett considered himself slick enough, but Donovan could match him, and his six-foot height seemed to go a long way in creating a dashing look.

Regardless of his extra height and debonair image, Donovan's judgment had been lacking lately, not only in the bicycle race today, but earlier, in his decision to send articles off to magazines with overinflated claims about the hotel. This wasn't the Donovan he had known for years. Bartlett would have to sit down and have an honest talk with him.

The sound of a key turning in the door between his office and Donovan's interrupted his thoughts.

Victoria felt a bit like Cinderella after the ball, having changed from Minette's gown into a plain skirt and waist. Her watch read two in the morning when she closed the door of Minette's suite behind her. Though she had tried to keep up a conversation with the French woman, who was obviously able to function well at this late hour, her thoughts had been on Rand.

Worried over what might happen with Donovan, she headed straight downstairs. In the deserted first-floor hallway, she was approaching the turn that would take her toward the suite of hotel offices when an elderly man stepped out of his room, struck a match, and drawing on a fat cigar, coughed up malodorous smoke directly in her path.

Victoria intended to step quickly past the resulting stench when she suddenly recognized the curly mop of graying hair, the thick brows and the drooping mustache.

She inhaled sharply. "Mr. Clemens!"

"Good evening." He glimmered at her from the narrow slits of his blue-green eyes, and drew again on his cigar.

Victoria opened her mouth to tell him how much she had enjoyed *The Adventures of Huckleberry Finn*, but, nearly choking on the fat smoke rings he emitted, could manage only a "Good evening, sir," before continuing on her way. Thankfully, Clemens was headed in the opposite direction.

Donovan's office was dark and empty, but the door to Rand's was open a crack. Through it drifted the assistant manager's distraught voice.

"... always got everything you wanted ... best jobs ... the only women worth having... tired of playing second ..."

Victoria approached Rand's door cautiously and peeked inside. Donovan's back was to her, but she could see that he was holding Rand in his chair with the aim of a small pistol while jamming the contents of the open safe into a satchel, a fistful at a time.

She listened to Rand's calm voice of reason. "Doesn't our friendship count for anything? We've been pals for more than fifteen years. I *know* you, Donovan. You're no thief. Besides, you'll never get away with this. I'm willing to forget this ever happened if you'll just hand me the pistol." He slowly extended his hand.

"Never!" Donovan ground out. "A groom has my mount ready, and at the docks, a yacht is ready and waiting. Once I've gone, you'll be done in this business, Bartlett!" With a vengeance, he stuffed another handful of currency into his bag.

Propelled by reckless, fiery anger, Victoria burst into Rand's office. "Mr. Donovan, how *could* you!"

Gun held chest high, he pivoted to face her.

Instantly, Rand bound over his desk, knocked Donovan's gun from his hand and swung at him, landing a right on his chin. Donovan staggered back, then regained his balance and took a fighter's stance.

Rand faced him, fists poised. "Give up, Donovan. You're no match for me. I knocked you silly plenty of times when we boxed at the club."

"I'll make you a loser this time, Bartlett!" He feinted a left, and when Rand moved to counter, hit him with a solid right, cutting him beneath the left eye.

Victoria winced for Rand, but he seemed to pay the bleeding no mind. He advanced, dodging Donovan's next swing and hitting hard to his body.

Donovan backed up, but Rand gave him no chance, quickly landing both fists to the head. The assistant slumped to the floor, unconscious.

Victoria hurried to Rand. "Are you all right? You're bleeding!" She gently pressed her handkerchief against his wound.

"I'll be fine," he assured her. He took a minute to catch his breath, then drew her hand from his cheek, pressing it to his lips. "Thank goodness you're all right, Tory. I don't know what I'd do if--"

"What the devil ...?"

Victoria withdrew from Rand quickly as Robert entered the office.

The bellboy sized up the situation with wide eyes that traveled from Donovan's still form, to Rand's cut cheek, to the pistol lying near the corner where it had landed during the scuffle. "I knew it!" he concluded excitedly. "I knew Mr. Donovan would be up to no good tonight, but you got the best of him, didn't you, Mr. Bartlett? Gol', tongues will really wag when word gets around--"

"Robert, you're to tell no one about what you've seen here," Rand stated firmly. "Tomorrow, I will explain to the staff what has happened. Now off with you."

"Yes, sir," Robert replied. Reluctantly, he headed out the door.

Rand held Victoria tenderly by the shoulders. "I should scold you for coming here tonight, but I'm so glad you're all right, I couldn't possibly do a convincing job of it."

Victoria gently pushed back the wave of hair that had fallen over his forehead. "I was too worried about you to stay away." She glanced down at the would-be robber. "Now that it's over, I feel a little numb."

Rand chuckled softly. "You can bet he does, too."

"What are you going to do with him, Rand?"

As he gazed at his friend, a look of sadness clouded his hazel eyes and etched a line in his forehead. "I'll have to turn him over to the authorities, but I'll request leniency for him." Taking Victoria by the elbow, he walked her to the door. "I'd see you to your room, but--"

"But you have your hands full right here. Are you sure I can't stay and help?"

He shook his head. "Go upstairs and try to get some rest. I'll see you later."

The following morning, Rand paced the carpet in front of his accountant's oversized desk. "What do you mean there isn't enough money, Munson? The hotel is packed. Every bed is filled, and several cots besides. Field day and the ball were successful by any definition," Bartlett raged.

"And well they should have been," Munson retorted. "You spent enough on them to entertain the queen and her court. I've spent this entire weekend paying cash to a procession of vendors who provided goods and services for your big affair."

"Cash?" Bartlett questioned sharply.

"Regardless of the articles that have appeared recently, the financial condition of Grand Hotel is no secret to the island merchants you've patronized. They know when to demand cash on delivery."

He held up a fistful of paid bills. "I warned you about your extravagances. It's your own fault the expenses overran the income. There is simply no possibility of paying Miss Whitmore the balance owed her until you provide further income to cover the amount."

Bartlett scowled. "Write the check, Munson."

The accountant opened his mouth to protest, but Bartlett cut him short.

"Just write it. I'll make good on it somehow before it's deposited."

He stalked out of Munson's office. Blast the accountant, anyway. He was too conscientious, coming in on a Sunday morning to work on the books. It could have waited another day. If only Munson had stayed home this morning, Bartlett would have written out Victoria's check himself and left Munson with the problem of juggling finances to make good on it.

Bartlett paused in Donovan's office on his way to his own. *Drat it!* The betrayal of his friend hurt him more than the possibility of explaining an empty safe. He had not realized jealousies had reached such absurd proportions on Donovan's part. The assistant had even admitted the trip he had sent Bartlett on to Petoskey early in the week had been an excuse to run Grand Hotel in the absence of its manager. He had used Munson as a lure, managing somehow to make the books at the Arlington look suspicious though nothing at all were amiss.

"Mr. Bartlett?" Munson's voice interrupted Rand's thoughts. "Here's the check you wanted." The accountant handed him a bank draft made out to Victoria. "What I really came for was to tell you how sorry I am to hear what happened with Mr. Donovan last night. I intended to mention it earlier, but we got caught up on the subject of bills and you left before I could say anything. Anyhow, I think it's a real shame." He shook his head slowly. "A real shame."

Robert must have spoken to Munson about the problem. Rumors are probably flying amongst the staff, and perhaps even the guests, Rand concluded.

"Thanks for your concern, Munson."

The accountant nodded, his jowls drooping even lower than usual when he left the room.

Alone again with his thoughts, Bartlett wandered into his own office, sat in the oversized desk chair, dropped the check onto the desk in front of him and stared at it. The sweet success he had hoped for from his big weekend had gone sour. Finances hadn't worked out. His best friend had turned on him. Tomorrow, Victoria would be gone, and he hadn't even the first notion how to cover her check.

Out of the black cloud came one pleasing thought. At least the contents of the safe were still intact, including Mrs. Palmer's $30,000 necklace and the manuscript Samuel Clemens had deposited there. Bartlett had been meaning to call on the author to make certain he had found his accommodations satisfactory. He hoped other guests had not intruded on the famous humorist's privacy and that he could proceed to the destination of his next lecture refreshed by his island sojourn.

Suddenly, a new thought occurred to Rand. He locked Victoria's check in his top desk drawer and headed in the direction of Clemens's suite.

"Are you *sure* they passed out all the fliers?" Bartlett asked Robert for the tenth time. "How do you know your young friends didn't just throw them in the nearest trash barrel?" He paced in front of the door to the nearly empty lecture hall. Only hours ago Samuel Clemens had decided, at Rand's suggestion, to delay his departure for Vancouver and give an evening lecture for the hotel's guests and other island visitors.

"They *didn't* throw them away. I'm sure of it," Robert insisted.

In an effort to spread word of the lecture, Bartlett had set announcements penned in Victoria's hand on all the tables at dinner. He had also paid a premium to the local printer to come in on a Sunday to make up fliers, and entrusted Robert with the responsibility of distributing them to the tourists on Main and Market Streets. In turn, the bellboy had enlisted the aid of some younger boys, none of whom was likely to be as dependable as Robert.

Now, with ten minutes to go until the start of the lecture, only Lily and Agatha Atwood had purchased tickets and taken seats in the lecture hall. Bartlett could feel the crushing weight of the ultimate humiliation coming down on him second by second.

Clemens would think Mackinac Island held a population of illiterates with no appreciation whatever for his humor and genius. Bartlett would bear the brunt of criticism from coast to coast once word got out that he had scheduled a performance for the renowned humorist but no one came.

"Mr. Bartlett, look!" Robert pointed to the knot of guests lining up behind the table in the foyer where Munson was selling tickets.

"Well, I'll be ..."

"I don't know why you were so worried. It isn't customary to show up ahead of time," Robert reasoned.

Indeed, Robert was correct. Bartlett had been so caught up in making arrangements for the affair, he had forgotten the social set often appeared at an event fashionably late.

"Remember what I told you, Robert. No one gets in without a ticket," Rand instructed.

Together, they stood at the door collecting tickets while Victoria, who had been overseeing arrangements backstage, came to usher guests to vacant seats. Within minutes the hall was filled to overflowing, and by the time Samuel Clemens began to speak, Munson was wearing a grin from ear to ear.

"You needn't worry about Miss Whitmore's check," the accountant whispered to Bartlett in the entryway. "I'll make a deposit first thing in the morning."

"Good, Munson. Thanks."

The accountant eyed him skeptically. "I don't know how you did it, but you made it rain dollars today."

Bartlett simply smiled.

Mr. Clemens's lecture ended at quarter past nine o'clock, but the guests remained for two hours at the reception being held in the parlor. By quarter past eleven, Victoria and Rand had managed to escort the guest of honor back to his first floor suite for a much-needed rest.

"I know it's late, Tory," Rand said, "but if you'd come to my office, I'd like to give you something."

Moments later, he held open his door for her, closing and latching it behind them. Ushering her to his desk, he opened the center drawer and withdrew the check, offering it to her with a flourish.

"Your long-awaited final payment, Tory." He laughed unconvincingly. "I wish I had thought to order champagne. I feel as though this momentous occasion requires some sort of celebration."

Though she had known it was coming, Victoria could hardly believe her goal had been accomplished and her days at Mackinac had finally reached an end. The realization sent a rock plummeting to the bottom of her stomach. She caught her lip between her teeth, and studied the check without really seeing it.

Taking a deep breath, she forced a smile, and raised her blue-gray eyes to his hazel ones, noting the lack of sparkle which had been evident only a few minutes earlier.

"Thank you. Now I can return home without fear of being labeled a complete failure." Her miserable attempt at humor fell flat and she turned her back to Rand, stashing the check in her skirt pocket, fighting desperately to retain her composure.

In an instant Rand closed the gap between them and turned her around to face him.

"I wish you didn't have to go," he quietly stated.

Victoria swallowed with difficulty. "We both know it is impossible for me to stay. Papa needs someone to help with the details he tends to neglect."

Chapter 14

"Someone, yes. But not necessarily you, Tory."

Victoria twisted out of his embrace, needing the perspective only distance can provide. "Please, Rand, let's not talk about it. I have to go home tomorrow." She nervously twisted the pearl ring about her left fourth finger. How she wanted to stay. In spite of her obligation to her Papa and Whitmore Furniture Manufactory, she might even consider staying, accepting his job offer, if only she could be sure once again that Rand had meant what he said the night he told her he loved her. But he had not mentioned love tonight.

"I understand," Rand said empathetically. The corner of his mouth turning up, he concluded, "I shall just have to limp along until I find a replacement for Donovan."

"I guess you shall," Victoria reluctantly agreed. Moving toward the door, she turned to face him again. "Will I see you tomorrow before I go?"

Rand looked up from the stack of papers he was shuffling on his desk. "I ... I'm not sure."

"Not sure?"

He ignored her quiet question, turning his attention again to the documents.

"I guess this is good-bye, then," Victoria managed in a small, steady voice before letting herself out.

Victoria rose early of necessity so she would have time to pack her trunk and eat breakfast before catching the ferry. In spite of the sunshine streaking in her window, her outlook was anything but bright. It seemed as though her heart were now wrapped in a dark shroud.

She had laid her pinstriped skirt out on her bed and was inserting tissue paper to prevent wrinkles when Lily's knock sounded. Victoria hurried to unchain and unbolt the door.

"I just had to come say good-bye." The pixielike wraith waltzed in barefoot, dressed in nothing more than her nightgown and robe. Her blue eyes were sparkling and her normally pouty mouth carried a pert smile.

"So tell me," Lily continued, "did RB keep his word, or is he sending you home destitute?"

"He kept his word," Victoria answered glumly, transferring the skirt to her trunk. Lily's innocent question served only to make her more distraught over leaving Rand behind.

"You needn't sound so enthusiastic," Lily jokingly chided. "I can understand your not wanting to go home. You'd be crazy to want to leave a man like RB when he's so obviously interested in you. So when are you coming back?" she asked casually.

"Coming back? No one said anything about coming back," Victoria responded curtly, secretly wishing she could know the answer to her friend's question.

"You needn't get touchy about it," Lily complained, "all I did was ask." She moved to the closet and began helping Victoria take shirtwaists off hangers. "That's it. You're grumpy because you're leaving today and you have no idea when you'll see the fabulous RB again, right?" She folded one of the waists with tissue and laid it in the trunk.

Victoria refused to comment. It irked her how intuitive and accurate Lily was in her perceptions.

The young girl continued, ignoring her friend's silence. "Well, I can certainly understand. I'll have only two more weeks with Auntie, then Parker and I will have to bid each other adieu until next summer."

Willing to hear of anything but Rand and leaving, Victoria picked up the thread of conversation. "For such a new friendship, it seems like you and Parker have taken quite a fancy to one another."

"Parker is *wonderful*!" Lily expounded, spreading her arms wide.

"But I shan't waste your precious last moments giving a discourse on his finer points. I'll help you pack." Lily waltzed to the closet. "Empty. Silly me. I should have known you had already finished the task, efficient as you are." She moved to the dresser. "Don't forget this, Tory." She held out the crystal perfume bottle Rand had brought as a gift earlier in the week.

Victoria had closed the lid on her trunk and was buckling the straps. She had already decided not to take his gifts with her, except for the pearl ring. She was wearing it now to keep from losing it, but she would take it off as soon as she found a good place to secret it away.

"You take the perfume, Lily. The contents would spill on the way home."

Lily's forehead wrinkled. "Are you sure, Tory? Rand gave this to *you*. Don't you want to keep it? I'm sure we can find a way to wrap it so it won't--"

"I'm sure." She buckled the second strap and rose to her feet. "And give this to Agatha for me," she said, offering her friend the heart-shaped foil candy box. "There are still a few pieces left."

"Tory, you're too kind. Auntie will love them. But she'd say exactly what I'm going to. Rand meant them for you."

Victoria simply shrugged, then turned to the mirror to put on her straw hat.

Lily inhaled sharply. "Tory, where did you get that ring?" She quickly set down the candy and perfume, taking Victoria's hand in hers to admire the pearl mounted on a circlet of gold. "He gave it to you, didn't he?" she breathed. "What does it mean? Are you engaged?"

Releasing her hand from Lily's, Victoria inserted a four-inch pin into her hat. "It doesn't mean anything. It was just another gift like the perfume and the candy."

"And the flowers," Lily added, scooping up a handful of rose petals that littered the dresser. She let them fall through her fingers. "But the ring is a gift you're definitely going to keep. Someday RB will replace it with a diamond," she predicted.

"I doubt that. Now, if you'll excuse me, I think I had better go downstairs and get something to eat." Victoria checked her watch. It read a few minutes past nine. Though her ferry wouldn't depart until eleven, it would take awhile to get served in the dining room, then present herself and her luggage at the docks.

"I guess this is good bye, then." Lily formed a pout, then hugged Victoria impetuously. She stood back, giving her friend a good looking-over. "I won't forget you, Tory. Don't be surprised if you hear from me. I'll write you in care of Whitmore Furniture Manufactory to the attention of the executive vicepresident, Miss Victoria Whitmore," she teased.

"I'll look forward to hearing from you, Lily. Thank you for all you've done. And Agatha, too. I'll always cherish her shawl. Please tell her for me. Now, I really must get downstairs."

In the hallway, Lily waited while Victoria locked her door. "Ta-ta, my friend." She made a parting gesture as she backed away.

"Good-bye, Lily." Victoria forced a smile that faded the moment her friend turned away.

The muffled clacking of steel against steel did little to lull Victoria to sleep as she rode the Grand Rapids and Indiana Line homeward bound. Her body was crying for rest. She couldn't get over how tired she felt once she had left Mackinac Island, but her berth in the sleeping car was cramped--shorter than her five feet six inches and very narrow--and her mind refused to surrender to the sweet oblivion of slumber.

It shouldn't bother her that she had seen nothing of Rand before leaving the hotel. He hadn't promised to see her off. In fact, he had refused to make any such commitment.

Her sense of loss, the realization she would not see him again, covered her with a mantle of loneliness nearly as burdensome as when she had faced her mother's death. To counteract the dull pain, she tried to look on the bright side.

Soon, she would be with her dear Papa and present him with the final payment. She wondered how he had fared without her. He could barely manage coffee in the kitchen, let alone a complete meal. She hoped he had taken his meals at the Eagle Hotel, a five-minute walk from the manufactory.

The apartment would undoubtedly be a clutter of cast-aside newspapers and books, dirty cups and glasses. If he had even been able to find his spectacles when he needed them, she would be surprised.

No need to worry that his clothes hamper would be overflowing.

Instead, she would find all his dirty socks, shirts, pants, and underdrawers on the floor right where he had dropped them.

Never mind. It would be good to see Papa again, feel him hug her when he met her train, smell the delicious mixture of wood shavings and cherry pipe tobacco on his skin and in his beard.

Yes, seeing him would be comforting, but it would not make up for the world she had left behind, the loneliness she struggled now to suppress. Gladly, she would deposit the check that would keep her father solvent for a few more weeks, months, a year? Proudly, she would accept his pat on the back, his, "A job well done, girl!"

With mixed feelings she would listen to the sequel. "I don't know what I'd do without you, Victoria."

He needed her. *Rand* needed her. Victoria loved both of them. Could she provide for both their needs? With startling clarity she recognized this as the key to finding a lasting happiness of her own.

No matter how difficult the circumstances, she had felt a sense of fulfillment in helping run her father's business, and the same feeling resulted when she was able to assist Rand at the hotel. Working with, or for, someone she cared about seemed essential to her own well-being, and she hadn't minded socializing with the wealthy patrons of Grand Hotel as much as she had expected. Minette had helped by accustoming her to their ways, and by the time the ball had ended, she had come to enjoy somewhat even the most formal social function.

Only the passage of time would answer Victoria's question of where happiness lay. Maybe Papa would learn to be more self-sufficient.

Not likely.

Maybe she would be able to forget Rand and Grand Hotel and Mackinac Island.

Even less likely.

Choices could be made. Or perhaps they would not be necessary. Would she ever hear from Rand again? Would she ever try to contact him?

The answers were possibly, and definitely not, respectively. Again, time.

Victoria had been welcomed with open arms when her father met her at the station, but she couldn't help wondering if the past week had only been a dream when she entered her father's apartment. It looked no different than when she had left for the train station. The tables in the living room were neat and orderly, the tidy kitchen could not have been cooked in, and when she reached her father's bedroom, she couldn't imagine where he had slept, his bed was so neat.

She crossed to the closet where he kept his hamper and opened the lid. Inside were a pair of trousers and shirt, both full of sawdust, and one set of dirty underwear, but no socks were strewn about, no undershirts draped over the bedpost, no indication whatever that the Jacob Whitmore she knew had been inhabiting his apartment.

Running a finger across his walnut dresser top, she checked for dust, but came up clean. This *was* puzzling. In a week's time, there should have been a thin layer distinguishable on the dark wood.

Hmm. He definitely had some explaining to do.

He had deposited her trunk and bag in her bedroom then returned to work in his workshop. Tonight, when he came upstairs for supper, they would talk. And he would tell her how he had acquired his black eye. He had brushed off her concern with a nonchalant, "Oh, that. I had a little problem. It's not worth mentioning."

In the meantime, she would unpack her belongings, visit the bank and the market, and prepare their evening meal.

"Victoria, this is the best steak I've had in I don't remember when," Jacob Whitmore repeated for the third time since they had sat down to dinner.

Unexpectedly, Victoria's father had left his workshop early to accompany her to the bank, then to market where, without explanation, he insisted on buying two of the finest steaks in the butcher's case. Now, they faced each other across the small kitchen table savoring tender, juicy morsels of meat, along with the fresh tomatoes, cucumbers, and melon she had picked out.

Most of their dinner conversation had consisted of Victoria's description of her experiences on the island with scant mention of Rand Bartlett until they had nearly finished their meal.

"I've been meaning to ask you, Papa, whatever possessed you to buy steak?"

He grinned sheepishly. "I thought you deserved it for all the effort you went to, collecting on Grand Hotel's account. Besides, a few of the suppers I cooked here while you were gone didn't exactly come out right, so I was hungry for a decent meal." He popped the last piece of steak into his mouth.

"You cooked?" Victoria asked, laying aside her napkin. "I thought from the looks of things, you had taken all your meals at the Eagle Hotel."

Jacob finished his lemonade and began clearing the table, an act she was witnessing for the first time. "I went out for the first few days, darlin', but their cooking can't compare with homemade, so by mid-week, I decided to cook for myself. I'll admit I've had to go some to get along here without you, but by golly, I managed."

"I should say so," Victoria agreed, wiping off the table while to her bafflement, her father tackled the dishes. Picking up a dish towel, she started to dry the clean china and silver.

"You also managed to get a black eye and avoid telling me how it happened. Now I want to know the truth."

He sighed. "I suppose there's no getting around it, is there? I might as well tell you everything, right from the beginning. The first few days you were gone, this place looked like a cyclone had struck. I couldn't even walk through a room without tripping over my own clutter."

He rinsed a plate and set it on the drain board. "One night, it was starting to get dark when I came home from dinner. I'd eaten a plateful of greasy fried chicken and some rock-hard biscuits and gravy that hadn't set right, then to make matters worse, when I walked into the apartment, I tripped over my own mess and struck the edge of the table. That's when I sat myself down and gave myself a talking to.

"I said, 'Jacob, you and this apartment have been in sorry shape since Victoria left, and there's no excuse for it. You're a grown man and it's time you took responsibility for your cooking and your clutter.'" He regarded her affectionately with his blue-gray eyes. "Till you went away, darlin', I hadn't realized how much picking up you did around here.

"As for my cooking, it will take me years to do as well at it as you do, but the very next morning I made myself some ham and eggs, and they came out passable, which is more than I can say for the slop they were serving down the street."

Victoria laid aside her towel to give her father a hug, planting a loud kiss in the middle of his bearded chin, and another on his cheek. Swallowing past the lump in her throat, she said, "Papa, you are really something, you know that?"

He dried his hands to embrace her, his chin resting on the top of her head. "And so are you, daughter. So are you."

Later, when the tiny kitchen was again spotless and every utensil returned to its proper place, Jacob sat down to read while Victoria slipped off to her bedroom.

She went immediately to the mahogany vanity her father had given her for her sixteenth birthday and opened the secret drawer he had built for hiding valuables. Until she had unpacked this afternoon the drawer had been empty. She took out the pearl ring and slipped it on her left fourth finger, remembering the evening Rand had given it to her and the magic she had felt whenever they were together.

A torrent of questions flooded her mind, unanswered, unanswerable, and she didn't hear her father coming until he spoke to her from the open doorway.

"A gift from an admirer?"

It was too late to keep the ring a secret. She went to him, holding her hand out for him to see. "From Mr. Bartlett."

He turned her hand this way and that. "A real beauty, isn't it?" His eyes, gray with a hint of moisture, left the ring and settled on her face. "Papa's darlin' is a grown young lady. I'm not surprised Mr. Bartlett noticed. I'd like to hear more about him when you're ready."

Victoria put her arm around his waist. "Let's go into the living room and talk, Papa ..."

She spent more than an hour speaking of the joys and frustrations she had experienced since her first meeting with Rand Bartlett, expressing her feelings as well as her concerns.

When she had finished, her father shared his own thoughts. "You're wiser than your years, Victoria, but I guess I've known that ever since your mother died. You say you believe time will tell how you and Mr. Bartlett really feel toward one another, and I'm sure you're right. I can only make one little suggestion. When the day comes you are certain of your feelings, act on them."

*   *   **

Minette's telegram came as a pleasant surprise one hot afternoon during the second week in September. Victoria had been to the lumber yard to see about a shipment of hardwoods and on her return, she found the message waiting for her on her desk.

The French woman was coming to Grand Rapids on business the next day and wanted to take her and her father out to dinner. She had docked the *Mademoiselle* at Grand Haven and would be coming in a hired rig to the city.

Victoria had not heard a word from Rand in three weeks. Though curiosity was gnawing at her, she vowed she would not initiate conversation about the man who appeared nightly in her dreams and daily invaded every moment when she was not concentrating on her father's business. She vacillated between feeling slighted, and reminding herself that correspondence--or was it only bill-paying?--was one of his weak points.

No doubt, too, Rand had been overworked with Donovan gone. Perhaps he was training a new employee for the position, or maybe he would let it go wanting until next season.

Throughout dinner at the Morton House, the most elegant restaurant in the city, Minette spoke of her plans to buy and renovate the River City Hotel, a hostelry in the heart of Grand Rapids that had seen better days. She had come with cash in hand to place an order with Whitmore Furniture Manufactory for the furniture, to be delivered when the renovation would be completed in the spring.

Following a lengthy discussion of the details of the contract, Jacob stopped by his workshop to find samples of various types of lumber while Minette and Victoria prepared coffee and dessert in the apartment upstairs.

Alone with Victoria, Minette wasted no time sharing news of Grand Hotel and its manager.

"Rand has become impossible!" she complained, setting forks and napkins on the kitchen table while Victoria sliced into the custard pie she had baked especially for her guest. "Since you left, he has been grouchy as, how you say? A grizzly bear? He criticizes mercilessly. Robert resigned a few days after you left, and Mr. Munson threatened to do so last week, just before I departed on the *Mademoiselle*."

Victoria lifted a wide slice of pie onto a plate and set it on the table.

"Has Rand hired a replacement for Mr. Donovan yet?"

Minette's eyes rolled. "No. And it is for the best. Rand is so cantankerous, a new employee would not be able to put up with him.

"It is a good thing there are no more guests for this season, only maintenance to be done. I hope the remaining staff does not walk out on him before the second weekend of October when he will close up the hotel." Minette casually slipped her hands into her skirt pockets. With a puzzled look, she removed a small envelope. Seeing Victoria's name penned on its face, she gasped. "I would be in deep trouble if I did not deliver this."

Victoria studied the tiny script written in black ink on the white vellum, Rand's penmanship. From the stairway, she could hear her father's footfalls. She slid the missive into her own skirt pocket. "I'll read it later."

Minette winked. "I shall be here long enough to enjoy your pie and lemonade, then I must be off again and you can read Rand's message in private."

Minette had not been long gone when Victoria repaired to her room to read Rand's note. Igniting the gas jet, she reached for the brass letter opener her mother had always used and with trembling hands tore a neat slit across the top of the heavy vellum envelope and extracted a note card. It bore Grand Hotel's insignia embossed in gold foil on the front. Inside was a train ticket from Grand Rapids to Mackinaw City and his brief message.

> Dear Tory,
>
> There is something very important of which I failed to remind you when I offered you the position as my assistant.
>
> I love you.
>
> With each passing day, my love for you increases.
>
> You already know I need you. The job is still open. I hope you will reconsider. RB

Chapter

15

Rand Bartlett leaned back in his oversized desk chair and gazed at the telegram. The smile playing at the corners of his mouth gave only a subtle hint of the relief he felt, knowing Victoria would arrive on the afternoon ferry.

He was glad he had sent her only a brief note reminding her he loved her. How he had wanted to write page after page of his need for her, of the depression her departure had caused, of the way almost nothing had gone right since the day she went away.

He could have told her how he had not been able to concentrate for his painful longing to be with her. He could have admitted how difficult he had become as a boss and told of his own blame for his bellboy resigning and his accountant threatening to do so.

He read Victoria's cable again. He need not worry that his feelings for her would go unrequited, for she had included on the last line three very important words, "I LOVE YOU." Soon, she would be on the island and he would be able to tell her the same in person.

The hands on his clock seemed to creep ahead, but at last it was time to meet her ferry at the dock. He stopped by his apartment for his overcoat and hat and headed out the back door toward the barn. A gust of wind nearly made off with his hat and he felt raindrops stinging his cheeks. He considered returning for his umbrella but decided the wind would only fold it inside out.

How quickly the storm seemed to be blowing in. He wondered if he would ever get used to the changable weather on the island. Occasionally he had heard stories from islanders of the dangers of straits weather, particularly in the spring and fall, but he had paid little heed. During his business trips to Petoskey and Detroit he had encountered rough weather only twice, and the ferry captain seemed equal to navigating the swells.

In the barn, the barouche stood rigged and waiting. As he drove toward the docks, Rand could hear the wind whipping through the treetops, rustling the leaves. Small, weak branches sailed down to litter Cadotte Avenue.

Out on the bay, choppy swells broke into whitecaps and gained height with the freshening wind. Waters that had been sparkling blue beneath yesterday's sunshine were turning murky gray to reflect the darkening sky above.

Though the barouche was extremely well-built, a stiff breeze rattled its braces and caused the canvas top to flutter. Rand brought the carriage to a halt near the pier for the Arnold Transit Line and scanned the straits waters, but found no sign of the Mackinaw City ferry that was due in three minutes.

Victoria braved the cold, wet breeze to stand alone at the port rail near the bow as the ferry pulled away from the dock at Mackinaw City. Unlike her previous trip to the island, she was the only passenger on deck. The straits were not glass calm, but undulating with swells, and seventy-degree temperatures had given way to a thermometer reading in the forties.

How things had changed since she had made that first ferry trip in mid-August. Her father had contracted enough orders and received sufficient cash down payments to keep him busy and financially sound for a year, and Jacob Whitmore himself had quickly learned how to tend to the bookkeeping once his daughter had shared Rand's note with him.

Except for the weather, which seemed to be growing increasingly stormy, Victoria could not have been happier to be on her way back to Rand. She could remember his face as though it were yesterday when she had last seen him--his widow's peak and the wave of hair falling down on his forehead, the hazel eyes sparkling with energy--she could even feel his strong arms around her and the press of his solid chest against her in an embrace. Her blood tingled with the thought of being near him again.

The ferry had not been long out of Mackinaw City when the wind stiffened, raising the swells higher and churning their crests into foam that sprayed her coat with cold droplets of water. Above, the hurrying sky grew darker and an ominous wind swung from northwest to north with increasing pressure, then quickly to northeast.

The bow of the *Algomah* plowed through high waves with a choppy rhythm. Overhead, dark clouds heavy with moisture began letting loose their bounty. Victoria abandoned her vantage point in favor of the enclosed deck lounge, choosing a wooden bench near the window overlooking the bow.

She sat alone. The tourist season on Mackinac had ended and few passengers required ferry services during the remainder of the year. Evidently no one else had bought passage on this crossing, though she had overheard talk in the Arnold Line office about the islanders looking forward to the arrival of the mail and other cargo aboard the *Algomah*.

Victoria tried to imagine how quiet the island would be. Only a small number of residents remained permanently, and few merchants and hotel-keepers would still be there to close up their establishments. The *Algomah* was making only one trip per day now, as were the Grand Rapids and Indiana trains from the city to the north country.

For several minutes, Victoria studied the movement of the ferry toward the island, and began to wonder if it were actually getting any closer. The increasing swells seemed to thwart its progress and unless she had been imagining things, the vibrations of the engine had dropped to a lower frequency, as if losing power, yet they were only about halfway to Mackinac.

A figure appeared on the deck outside the lounge, and she soon recognized the salt-and-pepper beard and ruddy, weathered face of Scotty. Despite the rocking motion of the ship, he quickly made his way to the lounge door, allowing a healthy gust of cold, damp air to enter with him.

He pulled the knitted tam from his head and swatted it dry against his thigh before replacing it at a jaunty angle on his silver hair.

"Scotty, do you remember me from last summer?" Victoria asked anxiously. "Miss Whitmore. We met on a crossing to Mackinac in the middle of August."

He stared at her a moment before his gray eyes began to sparkle with recognition. His mouth, drooping at one corner from the weight of a pipe, curved in a lopsided smile.

"Aye, lass, I surely do remember ye."

"Scotty, it seems like we're moving backward." She gestured toward the island, which appeared smaller than it had before the engines had lost power.

"Indeed, we are. The cap'n sent me to the tell the passengers--passenger, I mean--there's been a problem below. The main pipe burst. His crew's a-fixin' it though, so don't you fret. We'll be underway again soon enough."

"But Scotty, the weather. It's getting worse." She pointed to a line of thickening dark clouds to the northeast.

He gave a solemn nod and drew on his pipe, sending aromatic smoke rings into the air that drifted off lazily in comparison to the wind that was gusting against the lounge windows.

"There's dirtier weather ahead, no doubt. We'll be late making port, but we'll get there safe. You just hold tight, lass, and stay inside. I'm goin' below again to see if I can be o' any help to the boys." Pipe clenched between his teeth, he braved the cold air that blasted him the moment the lounge door opened, then worked his way along the port rail toward the stairs.

The motion of the *Algomah* in the rising waves made Victoria increasingly uneasy, with its heavy listing from starboard, to port, and back again. Her stomach grew queasy. *We'll be late making port, but we'll get there safe.* Surely Scotty must know what he was talking about.

Through the window, she caught a glimpse of the Mackinaw City shoreline. The *Algomah* had drifted so close she could pick out the rocks. If the vessel ran aground, surely the waves would break it apart. Panic raced through her. She made for the port window to get a better look, nearly losing her balance before she reached the railing. She was holding on with tightly clenched fists when Scotty again entered the lounge.

"Scotty, what's happening? Won't the engines work? Tell me, please!"

The old man laid a hand on her arm. "Come, lass. Sit down and calm yourself. Won't do a bit o' good to get into a dither. The pipe's nearly fixed." He helped her onto a bench. "You just hold tight and say a prayer for the cap'n an' his men." A moment later, he was gone.

"*Please*, Lord, let those men finish their repairs in time," Victoria prayed. Her sights on the shoreline, it seemed there could not possibly be enough water in the trough of the waves to keep the ferry afloat.

Then, the engines surged with new power, sending a welcome vibration through the floor and into her legs, along the bench and through her body. "Thank you, Lord," she whispered, cherishing the feel of the ship's power at work. The crisis past, she breathed a deep, relaxing sigh and watched the approach to the island.

The vessel continued its seesaw motion. In the worsening storm, waves sent spray onto the lounge deck against windows and doors. Victoria's stomach tightened as the feelings of nausea increased.

She tried to forget about the rocking motion and think of Rand and how wonderful it would be to see him once again, but her condition became more unsettled. The vessel pitched farther and farther with each wave. When she was certain she would vomit any second, she staggered toward the door.

The moment she unlatched it, the wind whipped it open, forcing her onto her knees. In the next instant, she was awash in the cold water that came spilling over the deck.

Soaked from head to toe, she struggled to her feet, her clothing heavy with lake water. When the *Algomah* listed in the opposite direction, she made for the low rail, throwing up into the churning waters before the next wave washed on deck.

Gripping the rail as tightly as possible, Victoria ducked her head while cold straits waves swamped her. Eyes shut, she felt her nose and mouth filling with water and her hold slipping as she began to float in the sea on the deck. In her mind, she saw herself washing overboard.

Dear Lord, no, she prayed, *please don't let it end this way.*

An hour had passed since Rand Bartlett had come to meet Victoria. Soaked from the driving rain, he nevertheless stood on the shoreline and searched the straits with the pair of binoculars he had borrowed from the agent in the Arnold Transit Line office.

In the distance he could see only towering waves and foam and dirty clouds moving in the direction from which the *Algomah* should appear. Even if she managed to enter the harbor, her captain would have a devil of a time bringing her to the dock where waves washed over the pier with each new swell and the gale-force wind would press against her hull like a sail.

With renewed force, a windy gust swept away Rand's favorite bowler, carrying it into the churning bay. Grumbling at the indignity, he pulled up his collar and headed for the ferry office.

Daylight had turned to dusk, and dusk to darkness. Filled with worry, Rand Bartlett paced the shoreline. In the black of night, no ship lights were detectable. Arnold Transit had tried to send out another vessel to assist the *Algomah*, but the size of the waves had prevented any boats from leaving the bay.

Had the *Algomah* gone down? She was a sturdy ship, fit for all kinds of weather, so the man at the ferry office had assured him. "She's unsinkable," he had said, though admitting this storm was more typical of a fierce November gale than of early October weather in the straits.

Where is the Alogmah? Rand wondered. If he lost Victoria now, he would never forgive himself for having asked her to come to him.

Then, the tiniest speck of light appeared on the horizon. Rand raised the binoculars. It was impossible for him to tell for certain whether it was the *Algomah*, but deep inside he was certain it must be.

For a long time, he watched the lights coming closer and listened to the storm. The winds were abating, the swells were pounding the shoreline with a little less force, but it would be a long time before the momentum of the storm had died down. He headed back to the shipping office.

The *Algomah* had passed back and forth for hours waiting for the storm to subside before entering the bay and attempting to dock. Dawn had broken, a dawn of heavy skies and rolling waters, but the fury of the gale had blown itself out leaving only the murky remnants of its nasty deed.

Rand stood on the pier along with several other men waiting to help tighten the lines and snug her alongside. It wouldn't be an easy task in this wind, but at least the swells had subsided so as not to wash over the pier.

As the ship came closer, he anxiously searched the deck for a glimpse of Victoria. He had hoped to see her waving to him from the rail, but she was not in sight.

He caught a line a crewman tossed him and began wrapping it about a pier piling. Others near him did the same. With a scrape and a bang, the gangway bridged the gap from ship to dock, but where was Victoria?

His heart suddenly froze. Something must have happened to her on the crossing. He was about to charge aboard the ferry and search for her when he saw her coming toward him on the arm of a weathered old sea dog.

Her tousled hair, her bedraggled coat, could not detract from the expression of joy on her face when she saw him.

Victoria gave Scotty's arm an affectionate pat before leaving him to join Rand. If not for the old captain, she would have found an early grave in the cold, churning waters. Thank goodness, he had come along the deck when he did, preventing her from washing overboard with a grip about her waist like a huge bear.

But her brush with death had passed, and she gazed now at the man she loved, cherishing the sight of his windblown hair and the look of relief in his tired, hazel eyes.

Quickly, Rand tucked her hand in his arm. "Thank goodness, you're finally here," he said, hurrying her away from the dock.

When they stood alone by the barouche, he held her chin tenderly in his hand and searched her blue-gray eyes. "Now that I've got you back, Tory, I'm never going to let you go. You can't possibly know the torture these last several hours have put me through, worrying about you, wondering if I would ever see you again, knowing if anything happened, I would blame myself forever for having asked you to come here." Gently, he pushed back a wet strand of her hair. "Tory, I love you. I want to marry you. Say you'll be mine for ever and ever."

She touched her finger to his brow, smoothing away the last remnants of worry. How thankful she was to be standing on solid ground, to be facing the man for whom she cared so deeply. "And I love you, Rand Bartlett. There were times when I wondered whether I would ever see your face again. Words cannot say how wonderful it is to be by your side. Nothing in the world could make me happier than to be your wife."

In an instant his arms were around her, a blanket of security holding her against his solid chest, telling her without words their love would last.

MORE ABOUT MACKINAC

For readers interested in Grand Hotel and Mackinac Island history, the following books provide excellent information:

Grand Hotel, Mackinac Island, John McCabe.

Mackinac, the Gathering Place, Russell McKee, editor.

Mackinac Island, Its History in Pictures, Eugene T. Petersen.

SEPARATING FACT FROM FICTION

Samuel Clemens actually visited Grand Hotel during August of 1895 at the invitation of the manager, James Hayes. The humorist's intention from the outset was to give a lecture.

In the early 1890's, the dynamic Hayes simultaneously managed the three hotels mentioned in the story.

Descriptions of Grand Hotel 1895 in this novel are as accurate as could be ascertained from available sources. When information was lacking, the author's imagination supplied details in keeping with the period.

The cover art accurately depicts the façade of the hotel for this period--without the flags and awnings. Outbuildings which stretched to the east of the main structure have been intentionally omitted.

For readers unfamiliar with Mackinac Island of today, horses and carriages still crowd its narrow streets during tourist season much as they did in 1895, because cars are not allowed.

ABOUT DONNA WINTERS

Donna adopted Michigan as her home state in 1971 when she moved from the Rochester, New York area. She began penning novels in 1982 while working fulltime for Lear/Siegler, Inc. (now Smiths Industries). She resigned in 1984 following a contract offer for her first book.

Her husband, Fred, an American History teacher, shares her enthusiasm for history. Together, they visit historical sites and restored villages, taking camera and tape recorder to capture a slice of America's past which she can share with her readers and he with his students.

Donna spent the summers of her youth at her parents' cottage on Lake Ontario, and has always lived in states bordering on the Great Lakes. Her familiarity and fascination with these remarkable inland waters and her residence in the heart of Great Lakes country make her the perfect candidate for writing *Great Lakes Romances*_{TM}.

ROMANCES BY DONNA WINTERS

Jenny of L'Anse Bay - June 1867 - A raging fire destroys more than **Jennifer Crawford**'s new home; it also burns a black hole into her future. To soothe Jennifer's resentful spirit, her parents send her on a trip with their pastor and his wife to the Indian mission at L'Anse Bay.

There, in the wilderness of Michigan's upper peninsula, Jennifer soon moves from tourist to teacher as she takes over the education of the young Ojibway Indians. Without knowing their language, she must teach them English. Without knowing their customs, she must live in harmony with them.

Meanwhile, **Hawk**, son of the Ojibway chief, teaches Jennifer the ways of his tribe. Often discouraged by seemingly insurmountable cultural barriers, Jennifer must also battle danger, death, and the fears that threaten to come between her and the man she loves.

Paperback, 5-3/8" x 8", 224 pages, $5.95.

Elizabeth of Saginaw Bay - When twenty-year-old **Elizabeth Brownell Morgan** arrives at Saginaw Bay with her husband, **Jacob**, a banker, to whom she has been married only a month, she regrets not heeding her cousin Agatha's advice to stay in New York. Where are the streets, the clapboard houses, the picket fences, and all the other signs of the thriving new town which had been described by Jacob's uncle before they purchased their village lot?

Set in 1837, *Elizabeth of Saginaw Bay* brings to life the exciting early days of Michigan's statehood, and the triumph of love over adversity in a rugged wilderness.

Paperback, 4-1/8" x 7", 196 pages, $2.50.

For the Love of Roses - (contemporary) - **Carey McIlwain** didn't need someone else to tell her about **Gavin Jack's** rude, abrupt behavior. She already realized how arrogant and unfair the handsome rose grower was to predict her failure in managing her parents' greenhouse business. Alex Hensley, on the other hand, was relaxed, courteous, and kind. He had been supportive when she felt insecure. She knew she was safe with Alex, but her heart was drawing her to Gavin...

  Paperback, 4-1/8" x 7", 188 pages, $2.25.

SOMETHING NEW FROM BIGWATER PUBLISHING

1990 Great Lakes Calendar - A Piece of History Each Day$_{TM}$ - Do you know how Detroit got its name, or when the first steamship was launched on the Great Lakes? Can you name the first European woman to live in Michigan, or the first to shoot the rapids at Sault Saint Marie? Answers to these questions and more can be found on the pages of this unique calendar. Fun and fascinating, it provides a constant source for stimulating dinner conversation; or tuck a page in your brownbag lunch (or your husband's or child's) for something new to share with lunch-mates. You'll never have a dull day with your *Great Lakes Calendar - A Piece of History Each Day*$_{TM}$. Makes a great gift--treat yourself and that special someone who has everything.

  Available July 1, 1989, 365 pages, $7.95.

ORDER FORM

Customer Name

Address

Available while supplies last.

Quantity			Total	
	Mackinac, $6.95			
	Jenny of L'Anse Bay, $5.95			
	Elizabeth of Saginaw Bay, $2.50			
	For the Love of Roses, $2.25			
	Available July 1, 1989 *1990 Great Lakes Calendar - A Piece of History Each Day*$_{TM}$ $7.95			
	Subtotal:			
	Postage - add $1 for first item, 50¢ for each additional:			
	Michigan residents include 4% tax:			
	Total:			

Send check or money order to:
Bigwater Publishing
Order Department
P.O. Box 177
Caledonia, MI 49316

READER SURVEY

Your opinion counts! Please fill out and mail this form to:

Reader Survey   Your Name:
Bigwater Publishing   Address:
P.O. Box 177   (optional)
Caledonia, MI 49316

If you include your name and address, we will send you a bookmark and the latest issue of our *Great Lakes Romances*_{TM} *Newsletter.*

1. Please rate the following elements from 1 (poor) to 5 (excellent):

_____Heroine   _____Hero   _____Setting   _____Plot

Comments:_____

_____

2. What setting (time and place) would you like to see in a future book?

_____

3. Where did you purchase this book?

_____

4. What influenced your decision to purchase this book?

_____Publicity (Please describe)_____

_____

_____Front Cover   _____First Page   _____Back Cover Copy

_____Title   _____Friends   _____Other (please

describe)_____

5. Please indicate your age range:

_____Under 18   _____25-32   _____46-55

_____18-24   _____35-45   _____Over 55